D0753927

SCENES OF JEWISH LIFE IN ALSACE

The Between Wanderings collection

These new translations of vintage books celebrate Jewish life from the 1850s to 1920s—a time of intense migration, changes and challenges for Jews around the world. Some of the books feature first-person accounts describing the era's Jewish communities, customs, folklore, synagogues, schools, foods and culture.

1. *Sephardic Jews and the Spanish Language* — Nonfiction by Ángel Pulido

2. *Jewish Immigrants in Early 1900s America: A Visitor's Account* — Photo booklet; text by Anatole Leroy-Beaulieu

3. *Scenes of Jewish Life in Alsace: Village Tales from 19th-Century France* — Stories by Daniel Stauben

For news of upcoming fiction and nonfiction releases, visit betweenwanderings.com.

SCENES OF JEWISH LIFE IN ALSACE

Daniel Stauben

Illustrations by Alphonse Lévy

Translated by Steven Capsuto

Steven Capsuto
Books & Translation Services
New York

This book was first published in French in 1860 by Michel Lévy Frères under the title *Scènes de la vie juive en Alsace*.

English translation copyright © 2018 by Steven Capsuto.

All rights reserved. No part of this book may be reproduced, distributed or transmitted in any form or by any means without written permission. Please address permission requests to the copyright holder at the address below.

Steven Capsuto
P.O. Box 194, New York, NY 10113
steven@betweenwanderings.com

Between Wanderings books and blog:
betweenwanderings.com
@BWJewishHistory

Front cover: James Rollins Design.
Illustration adapted from an Alphonse Lévy etching.

Back cover: Photograph of Auguste Widal by Antoine Meyer, published 1884.

Book Layout © 2017 BookDesignTemplates.com.

**Scenes of Jewish Life in Alsace/
Daniel Stauben (tr. Steven Capsuto). -- Edition 1.5.**

ISBN 978-0-9978254-7-3

Contents

Translator's Preface

AUGUSTE WIDAL ("DANIEL STAUBEN") was born in 1822 in a rural Yiddish-speaking community in France. That was a time of dizzying change, just thirty years after France abolished its national anti-Jewish laws, and four years after it lifted similar regulations in the author's native region, Alsace. Jews in French cities were starting to integrate into society, but village life in Widal's region was more insular. In that shtetl-like orthodox world, nearly everyone spoke Yiddish and many Jews knew little French. Their culture was suffused with a mix of country customs, devout religiosity, and old folklore rich in legends of ghosts and sorcery and of "wonder rabbis" who could banish demons and lift curses.

Widal's father wanted him to be a rabbi, but young Auguste's passion was classical literature. By the time he started drafting these "Scenes of Jewish Life," he was a doctoral student in Paris. In that urban secular environment, Widal had grown nostalgic for his childhood village of Wintzenheim and decided to write some stories set in Alsace. He took inspiration from George Sand's pastoral novels, but instead of Sand's Christian peasants, he wrote about Jewish family life, celebrations, foods, courtship, songs, prayers and folk tales.

From 1849 to 1853, the Jewish magazine *Archives Is-raélites* published the tales that would become the first half of this book. Widal composed the early stories as letters to the editor, describing recent visits home after a long absence. It is unclear whether he truly took all those trips or if he drew on boyhood memories of the 1820s and 1830s. I suspect it was largely the latter, since the first installment attracted irate letters from Alsatian Jews. They said that the story—warmly received elsewhere in France—had unfairly portrayed modern Alsatians as ignorant, superstitious yokels. An editor's note accompanying the second story replied:

> Certainly, if the author has any intent beyond the purely literary, it is a clear wish to pay loving homage to the timeless traditions of the old Jewish rural life; to exhume some poetic legends, to describe certain customs and manners that are disappearing quickly... To those who cry "false," Mr. A. W. could, if necessary, point to and name the models who posed for him; he himself lived enough years among those ancient customs to have observed and studied them in depth.

Widal reworked the stories twice for a more mainstream audience. In 1857 and 1859, the magazine *Revue des Deux Mondes* published a revision of the original letters plus additional stories set during Jewish holidays, and an 1860 book adaptation expanded the previous stories and added new tales. In these revisions, Widal adopted the pen name Daniel Stauben and added explanations of Jewish concepts for his new, mainly Gentile readers. Unfortunately, he also deleted much of the Jewish vocabulary that had given the tales their flavor. In the rewrites, for example, the village *hazzan* (cantor) became an *officiating minister*, and *Sukkoth* became the *Feast of Tabernacles* or *Feast of Booths*. Even the word *Yiddish* vanished, replaced by *Judeo-German patois* and *our incorrect but lovely and evocative Judeo-Alsatian jargon*. The present English translation reinstates most of the original Yiddishisms and Jewish terms for the sake of clarity and authenticity, alternating them with the generic equivalents. The text explains all these terms and, unless otherwise specified, all footnotes are the author's.

Widal's Jewish terminology reflects a blend of rural and urban influences, and this translation aims to preserve those inconsistencies. As a child, he would have called holidays by their Alsatian Ashkenazic names, such as *Shefuess* (Shavuos). After years in Paris, though, he began to spell them in a "scholarly" way influenced by Sephardic Hebrew. This English edition mirrors that with spellings such as *Shavuoth*. Widal also sometimes uses words from his childhood languages: Alsatian Yiddish (*shadshen, barches, fralleh*, etc.) and Ashkenazic Hebrew (*boruch habo, boi b'sholem*).

In transliterating the Yiddish, I have chosen spellings meant to convey the pronunciation to the average English reader: for instance, *kalleh* instead of the YIVO-standard *kale* (which most readers would pronounce like the vegetable), *shammes* instead of *shames*, and the regionalism *yontof* instead of *yontev*. This also applies to character names: Salomon's brother is *Yekel* in this edition, replacing the French phonetic *Iékel*. Bear in mind

that there is no silent E in Yiddish: the name *Yedele* is
"*Yeh*-deh-leh." The CH is a guttural sound, as in the Scot-
tish or German *Ach!* The combination EY rhymes with
hey, while AY rhymes with *sky*.

Why did Widal, a busy professor of classics and modern languages, keep expanding and promoting these
quaint, non-academic stories even once he was engrossed
in scholarly work? In the introduction to the 1860 book,
he explains:

> We have done our best to depict this sort of contempo-
> rary "Jewish antiquity" that is, sadly, about to vanish; for
> if the century stays on its current course (helped along by
> "progress" and railroads), within a few years, there will be
> no trace of these long-preserved ways of life. In more than
> one place, it is already fading away like all things that
> grow old. So let us urgently record its most characteristic
> traits.

A contemporary of Widal's felt this same urgency: the
artist Alphonse Lévy prolifically captured Alsatian Jewish
scenes in his paintings, drawings and etchings. Though
created for other purposes, Lévy's images line up with
Widal's stories with startling precision and add a touch of
whimsy to this edition. Most of these illustrations come
from Léon Cahun's 1886 book *La vie juive*, Lévy's own
1902 book *Scènes familiales juives*, and a series of Lévy
postcards published around 1900. The only non-Lévy illustration is the portrait of Rabbi Hirsch, from an
uncredited nineteenth-century print.

As Maurice Samuels points out in *Inventing the Israelite* (a book about French Jewish fiction), some scholars now credit Widal as "the initiator of a new form of 'ghetto nostalgia' that took hold in French and German literature and art after the Revolution of 1848" (p. 194). Widal himself knew he was treading strange ground with these stories. He devotes much of his introduction to justifying the subject matter and comparing it to the subjects of Sand's *The Devil's Pool* and *François the Waif*:

> I told myself that Berry is not the only part of France whose population boasts distinctive types, age-old customs and picturesque language. The peasants of Indre have counterparts... [in] the Jews of our Alsatian hamlets. Entrenched in the region since centuries before the French conquest, have they not preserved their own distinct language and lived their own distinct life? A life that differs from their Christian neighbors' lives as much as it differs from the experiences of urban Jews? Again I asked myself: Does Jewish Alsatian village life not offer a curious set of ideas, rituals, ceremonies, superstitions, folkways, rural archetypes and periodic festivals that, taken together, form a kind of civilization arising both from ancient belief and from the harshness of the Middle Ages and persecution? An intriguing spectacle, surely, for the philosopher and the artist!

It is time for us to behold that spectacle and meet Salomon, Yedele and their family and friends. Let us join our narrator on one of France's very first railway lines, as he crosses the eastern plains on his way to *Shabbes* dinner.

Steven Capsuto
New York
May 2018

Shabbes fish.

PART I

CHAPTER ONE

*Papa Salomon. — Friday evening; the Shabbes Shueh.
— The village of Bollwiller and its people. — Papa
Salomon's home and family. — Prayers and a meal.
— Samuel the storyteller.*

IT WAS NOVEMBER OF 1856. An invitation from an old friend brought me back to Alsace, to scenes of village life I had known first as a small boy and which I now witnessed again years later with great emotion. As it happened, this short first trip gave me a chance to observe not only the curious characters who populate rural Jewish society in Alsace, but also some striking religious rituals: Friday's and Saturday's Sabbath observances, followed by a wedding and later a funeral. These episodes all happened in the order presented here. Imagination played no part in the many events I shall narrate.

The village of Bollwiller, with its large Jewish population, lies a short distance from Mulhouse. Bollwiller is home to Papa Salomon, a handsome old man of seventy whose face exudes wit and warmth. Papa Salomon was to be my host, so I set out from Mulhouse to Bollwiller one Friday afternoon late enough to avoid reaching the village before around four o'clock. Arriving earlier would have disrupted their preparations for *Shabbes*—the Sabbath.

On Fridays, women and girls in Jewish villages do double duty: the Laws of Moses forbid handling fire on the Sabbath, and so besides supper they must also prepare meals for the next day. As I still recalled, Friday mornings and afternoons are hard work, but the evening is one of those rare moments of rest when a Jewish community fully displays its true spirit. For these good folk, when the last rays of the Friday sun fade, so do all the worries, all the sorrows and all the troubles of the week. People say that the *Danyes Vage* (Wagon of Worries) travels through the hamlets each night, leaving the next day's allotment of grief on poor humanity's doorstep. But they also say that this wagon, a painful symbol of country life, halts on Fridays at the edge of each village and will not rattle into motion again until the next evening.[1] Friday is everyone's night of joy and ease. This is when the unhappy peddlers that you see all week with a staff in their hand and a bundle of merchandise—their whole fortune!—bending their back as they trudge up hills and down valleys, living on water and brown bread... On this evening, without fail, those peddlers will have their *barches* (white bread),[2] their wine, their beef and fish. In summer, they will lounge in the doorway of their home in shirtsleeves and slippers, and in winter, they will sit behind a nice hot stove in a jacket and a cotton cap. On a Sabbath Eve,

---

[1] The Sabbath begins Friday evening. In Judaism, the evening before a holiday is celebrated like the holiday itself.

[2] Translator's note: *Barches* or *berches* means "challah." The author calls it white bread to distinguish it from the coarse brown bread that poor Jews ate on weekdays.

Shabbes in the village.

yesterday's deprived peddler would not change places with a king.

I arrived in Bollwiller just at the *Shabbes Shueh*: the Sabbath Hour. That is what we call the hour before people go to synagogue. It is when girls touch up their grooming, a bit disarrayed by the day's extra chores. It is also when fathers, fully dressed except for their frock coat, await the signal calling everyone to prayer. They use this free time to light the wicks of the seven-spouted lamp that all Jewish families have in Alsatian villages, made expressly for them as a fairly faithful replica of the famous ancient seven-branched lampstand. As I walked down the main street, I saw such lamps being lit in several homes. Suddenly, I heard the periodic banging of a hammer at different distances: three knocks on a shutter here, three knocks on a carriage gate there, struck by the *shuleklopfer*[3] in ceremonial dress. This signal was as effective as the liveliest pealing of the loudest bell. Groups of men and women left at once for services in their *Shabbes* best, a garb specific to our Jewish villagers: The men wear loose black trousers that nearly cover their big oiled boots, a huge but very short blue frock coat with oversized lapels and a massive collar, a hat that is narrow at the base and widens towards the top, and a shirt of coarse but white fabric. The shirt bears two collars so tremendous that they block the face entirely, and so starched that these fine people must turn their body to look left or right. The women wear a dark gown, a large red shawl

---

[3] One who calls people to synagogue by knocking. In Jewish ritual, bells are unknown.

The *shuleklopfer* (synagogue knocker).

adorned with green palm leaves, and a tulle cap laden with red ribbons. A band of velvet takes the place of their hair, which has been carefully concealed since their wedding day. This finery is completed by a beautiful *tefilleh* (prayer book) printed in Rodelheim[4] and bound magnificently in green morocco leather, which every pious woman holds majestically against her abdomen.

Soon I found myself alone in the street. I would gladly have gone straight to my host's house, but who could be so rude as to arrive at a home in a Jewish village on a Friday evening without going to synagogue first? So I ran there—a little ashamed at my lateness, I must confess. My host, waiting at the synagogue door, seemed to sense my embarrassment. He walked towards me, held out his hand and said the usual friendly "*Sholem aleichem.*"[5]

"Don't worry, my dear Parisian friend," he added. "You're not late at all. I knew you were coming, so I asked the *hazzan* (prayer leader)[6] to be patient for a few moments and not chant the *Boi B'sholem* until your arrival, which I trusted would be soon."[7]

I was touched by this religious courtesy and thanked my host for it.

---

[4] A town that, like Soultzbach, is famous for its printers of Hebrew books.

[5] "Peace be with you!"

[6] Officiating minister, cantor.

[7] These are the first two words of the Friday evening prayer. Once this prayer is said, the holy day begins. [Translator's note: These words actually begin the final verse of the hymn "L'cho Dodi" and mark the moment when the congregation welcomes the Sabbath into the synagogue.]

Like all houses in the village, Papa Salomon's home consisted of a ground floor, used as a shop, and an upper level where the family lived. Narrow, almost vertical stairs—strewn with red sand and lit by a sort of branched tinplate candlestick on the wall—led us to a front door adorned with a large *mezuzah*.[8] My host was a family man: his wife approached me, followed by two pretty daughters with very dark eyes and hair, and three vigorous lads. The whole brood laughed as they greeted me. In these Alsatian villages, people always laugh when welcoming guests, especially if they are afraid you will talk to them in French. This lets them be pleasant while stalling for time. The precaution was unnecessary in my case, since I am as proud as anyone to be a very correct speaker of our incorrect but lovely and evocative Judeo-Alsatian *Yiddish* jargon.

While Papa Salomon and his sons chanted the *Malke Sholem*[9] and the rest of the family listened in religious silence, I ran my eyes over our surroundings. I gazed happily at all these objects that are much the same in every well-to-do Jewish home, objects I had seen often as a child and which had retained their ancient simplicity. There was the obligatory lamp hanging from the ceiling, and a red chintz tablecloth under which a bulge near the big leather armchair betrayed the presence of two *barches* (loaves of white bread) ordered for Friday evening. In one

---

[8] A small tin case attached to a doorpost. It contains parchment on which is written the most important prayer of the Jewish faith, which begins: *Hear, O Israel, the Lord our God is one*, etc.

[9] One of the religious songs sung after returning home from synagogue. [Translator's note: Now usually known as "Sholem Aleichem."]

They lived on the upper level.

corner, a cistern with a copper basin rested on a green wooden base whose bottom, a cabinet, was reserved for storing the prayer book and some Talmudic volumes. One wall, the eastern wall, displayed a big, carefully framed sheet of white paper bearing the Hebrew word *Mizrach* (East). *Mizrach* signs are a common, thoughtful aid to visitors, letting them know which way they are commanded to face when praying to the Lord. Two prints also graced the walls: One depicted Moses with two rays of light shining from his forehead, with the tablets of the Law on his right and his classic staff on his left. The other portrayed the high priest Aaron, his chest and shoulders covered by the *koshen* and the *ephod*,[10] his head wrapped in a priestly turban. A small mirror hung below an enormous deer head that served as a rack for the master's hat or his cotton cap, depending whether he was at home or not.

After a meal of succulent Alsatian dishes, preceded and followed by prayers and psalms that Jews sing to traditional melodies, Papa Salomon told me that there would be a wedding the next Wednesday. His brother Yekel's son was marrying the daughter of a *parness*[11] in Wintzenheim, a village located one league from Colmar.

"My brother Yekel, who you'll see tomorrow," he said, "will invite you to the wedding. But tonight in your honor, we'll stay home. Do you still love stories around the fireside as much as you used to? Papa Samuel, who often spends Friday evenings here, will be with us tonight. Now

[10] Exodus 28:4.
[11] President of a Jewish congregation.

there's a storyteller! Ask my wife and children. It's amazing how much he has read and, more impressively, how much he remembers! Ordinary tales, extraordinary tales, legends, adventures, enchantments... just tug his sleeve and it all tumbles out. But allow me one comment, my dear *orech* (guest). I know that you Parisians put little stock in the supernatural. Think what you like, but if Samuel tells us a tale of magic, don't look skeptical. Otherwise he'll stop and get angry. He's proud in his way."

Just then we heard a heavy tread on the steps. The door opened without anyone knocking.

"*Gut Shabbes bay aynander!*" said a hearty voice: Samuel was wishing us a good Sabbath.

He looked to be about fifty. Long side-whiskers framed his intelligent, rather plump face. Like so many men in the Alsatian countryside, Samuel did a wide range of jobs.

This worthy neighbor of Papa Salomon's excelled equally in such varied and sensitive roles as substitute *hazzan* in the synagogue, nurse, storyteller, barber, matchmaker and messenger.

The new arrival, clearly aware of his status, settled in squarely and familiarly next to the master of the house.

"Samuel," said my host without further preamble, "your timing is perfect. Since we can't gamble tonight,[12] you'll tell us a *manze* (story), but a very good one to please this gentleman. This is a friend who lives in Paris."

Samuel nodded a greeting without touching his hat.

---

[12] Among Jews, it is forbidden to play cards on the Sabbath.

A Friday evening.

"I don't usually need coaxing," he replied, "but let me think a bit. Let's see! Now what could I tell you?"

His whole audience then launched a veritable assault on Samuel's repertoire and erudition. The lady of the house clamored for the legend in which the Queen of Sheba travels through Bollwiller at certain times of year at one in the morning, dressed in white, hair fluttering, seated on a golden chariot that propels itself without a team.

Salomon's two daughters begged Samuel to tell the tragic tale of little Rebecca, who unwisely glanced out her small kitchen window on a Saturday night. She saw the infamous *Mohkalb*[13] and heard its roar as it lurked beneath the outdoor sink, and she died of fright.

My host's sons pleaded for the adventures of old Jacob, who got lost on his way to the Saint-Dié fair. At three in the morning, after walking all night, he found himself back where he had started the evening and was chased home by a gang of *flame men*,[14] whose blazing fingers burned marks into his door as a sinister threat.

Papa Salomon asked for the story of notorious Nathan, known as *Nathan the Devil*, the terror and shame of the pious town of Grussenheim. Through his pacts with Hell, Nathan had conjured the sound of chimes in his granary in full view of everyone. He had made mysterious letters rain down from the ceilings and made tongues of flame

---

[13] A well-known legendary monster covered in eyes, also known as a *Dorfthier* (village beast).

[14] In German, *feurige Männer*. *Flame men* are clearly just a poeticized form of will-o'-the-wisps.

shoot from the four walls of the parlor, which burned without being consumed.[15]

"You've already heard all those tales or parts of them," Samuel said, raising his head up high. "Let me tell you one that's strange in quite a different way. I've never told it to anyone and I'll ask you to keep it strictly between us, for my safety and for yours."

"Before starting," said my host, "take this glass of wine, Samuel, and make a toast with this gentleman."

Then turning to the lady of the house, Papa Salomon said, "Yedele, call in the *Shabbes goye* (Sabbath maid)[16] to pour oil in the lamp, fix the wicks and stoke the fire." And resting his chin on both hands and his elbows on the still-open book of Psalms, he added, "Go ahead, Samuel. We're listening."

Samuel gulped down the wine, not without first reciting the required prayer,[17] and readjusted his hat (which he had kept on in the house, like everyone else, of course). Then, in a patois that unfortunately loses much in translation, he began his tale.

---

[15] The tale of Nathan is famous in the Jewish world of the Haut-Rhin. In the little village of Grussenheim, three leagues from Colmar and not far from the Rhine, devout people even today will fearfully show you the ruins of his house.

[16] A non-Jewish woman who, in every Jewish family, handles work forbidden to them by the commandments during those twenty-four hours.

[17] A prayer that country Jews always say in Hebrew before drinking: "Blessed art Thou, O Lord our God, King of the Universe, who bringeth forth the fruit of the vine."

A Jewish peddler on the road.

CHAPTER TWO

The tale. — A minor dispute. — Saturday daytime and evening.

"THE STORY I'M GOING to tell you happened long ago, maybe forty years ago, to my grandfather. You young people never knew him but you remember him well, don't you, Papa Salomon?"

Papa Salomon nodded.

"Grandfather was not rich. He lived like me, from day to day, and like me he did a little of everything. One Saturday evening in the dead of winter, an hour into the new week,[1] he happened upon big Hertzel.

"'A good week!' said Hertzel.

"'A good year!'[2] replied my grandfather.

"'Yudel, here's a chance for you to make some money.'

"'That suits me.'

"'But you'll have to spend the night away from home.'

"'I don't mind.'

"'My wife and I are expected in Herrlisheim on Monday morning to visit my brother-in-law, Isaac. His baby boy turns eight days old the day after tomorrow and

---

[1] For Jews, the new week begins on Saturday evening.
[2] The standard exchange of greetings.

we're supposed to be the godparents.[3] But my wife has been in bed with a fever for two days and I can't leave her. We must get word to my brother-in-law so he'll have time to find other godparents. As you see, I waited till the last minute. If I mail a letter, it won't arrive in time. I'd rather entrust it to you, Yudel. You'll deliver it to Isaac. Here, take this hundred-sous coin, and when you get back I'll pay you another.'

"'It's a deal.'

"'Good!' thought my grandfather. 'It's eight leagues from here to Herrlisheim but I'm a strong walker, so I'll make it in six hours. Six hours there, six hours back, one hour's rest... that's thirteen hours. If I leave now, I'll be home by eight in the morning and I'll have earned enough for a real feast next Friday evening.'

"'Give me my leather-trimmed trousers,' he told my poor old grandmother, 'my double-soled shoes, my gaiters, my tunic and my old cloak. Don't forget my *tefillin*,[4] which I'll need for morning prayer. I'll do that on the way back.'

"Weeping, my grandmother gave him all these objects.

"'Why the boo-hooing?' he asked. 'Don't you want to see me earn something?'

---

[3] The Jewish baptism is the *bris mileh* (circumcision), performed eight days after a boy is born. The godmother carries the baby in her arms to the door of the synagogue, and inside the godfather holds him in his lap during the procedure.

[4] Long leather straps wrapped around the right arm and around the head during morning prayer. A hollow on each strap holds a piece of parchment bearing the same prayer found in *mezuzahs* (Deuteronomy 6:4-10). Jews thus comply with the precept: "Thou shalt bind (my words) for a sign upon thy hand, and they shall be as frontlets between thine eyes" (Deuteronomy 6:8).

Wearing *tefillin* during morning prayers.

"'Yes, but I don't like you going out on a Saturday evening. I tell you it's dangerous to travel on Saturday evenings.'

"My grandmother was not wrong: Unfortunately, Saturday evening is when *he*[5] makes mischief and the *Mohkalb* is heard bellowing. After all, it was a Saturday evening when the serving girl at Elie's inn dared to look in the mirror and saw two big blazing eyes behind her, and an invisible hand struck and disfigured her. It was a Saturday evening when Sarah's son was caught up in a whirlwind and was nearly carried off by *sheydim*.[6] The boy could hear the unseen demons jumping and shouting all around him. He freed himself only by striking into the swirl of dust with his stick, which came out stained with blood. But what terrified my grandmother most was that the route from Bollwiller to Herrlisheim ran through a certain little meadow. Now, in this little meadow were some trees, and at the foot of these trees, some turf. And on this turf, here and there, were small circles where grass would not grow. And the grass would not grow there because it was burnt to the root. And it was burnt because it had been trampled at certain times of night. And what had burned it was the *machshovim*.[7] But grandfather was no coward.

"'Nonsense!' he said. 'I've traveled at all hours of the night and no one has eaten me yet. I'll be back in no

---

[5] The *Devil*. Common folk take care not to utter this word, especially at night.

[6] Hebrew word meaning "demons."

[7] Hebrew word meaning "sorcerers."

time, and then with the hundred sous that big Hertzel gave me, I'll go and buy potatoes from our neighbor Mey (Marie), who sells them very cheaply.'

"As I mentioned, this was winter. It was February and the cold was intense. Snow had fallen for days, frozen to the ground and gleaming in the distance in the moonlight. It was a good walk. My grandfather walked more than five hours, letting nothing, absolutely nothing, slow him down.

"'Another three-quarters of an hour,' he thought, 'and I'm there.'

"In fact, he could already see the wall around the little meadow. As he reached the short stone bridge opposite the white wall, the Herrlisheim clock struck eleven thirty. He stopped, thinking he'd heard a strange noise. Turning this way and that, he saw nothing and decided he'd been wrong. When his journey brought him at last to the foot of the white wall, he stopped again. There was no mistake this time: it sounded like feet treading the ground, and his ear was struck by wild shrieks and by bursts of laughter."

Here, Samuel broke off. His listeners all let out a "*nohn*?" whose meaning was unmistakable. In our Judeo-German patois, *nohn*[8] is an expression of impatience that means something like "Keep going, don't stop just when it's getting good! What happened next? Go on! Continue!"

Visibly pleased, the old fellow resumed his tale.

---

[8] Translator's note: An Alsatian pronunciation of the Yiddish word *nu*. Here the author inserts a note that says, "From the German word *nun*." Some reference books do trace *nu* back to German, while others link it to Slavic languages.

"As a precaution, my grandfather gingerly took his *te-fillin* from his pocket and out from under his cloak, and was striding around the corner of the little wall when suddenly, his eyes beheld... What?... About twenty wild-haired old women wearing nothing but their shifts, holding hands and dancing in a circle in the snow, uttering strange words to a disturbing rhythm. Whirling in the middle of their circle, a similar figure held in her emaciated arms something resembling a baby doll that she would toss to the others, who would catch it and throw it back, one after the other. Anyone but my grandfather would have been paralyzed with fear. He, however, kept his head. Our former Chief Rabbi Hirsch, whose portrait you have right here, a great *bal-Kabolleh* (scholar of Kabbalah), had once told my grandfather how to exorcise apparitions. Grandfather remembered this and said some magic words that he would never teach to anyone, not even me, and then he threw his *tefillin* into the middle of the commotion. The entire hideous troupe transformed into as many black cats, which climbed nearby trees where clothes fluttered in the breeze. In these garments, the old women then resumed their true shape, stood still and silent for several moments, and after a few minutes, they vanished.

"As you can imagine," continued Samuel, "my grandfather covered the remaining distance to Herrlisheim speedily after snatching up his *tefillin*. Grandfather was not walking now but running. He reached the edge of the village twenty minutes later. In front of Isaac's home, at that late hour, he was shocked to see groups of men and women in front of the door, whispering to each other. Grandfather walks through the crowd and into Isaac's house. He finds everything in chaos.

"Isaac was pacing and talking to himself. 'Such tragedy and joy at the same time! No! This is not natural at all!'

"'I've come from Bollwiller,' said my grandfather, approaching him. 'Here is a letter for you. It's urgent.'

"Isaac read the letter.

"'My God!' he cried. 'We very nearly didn't need godparents at all.'

"Isaac told my grandfather what had happened. Earlier that night, Isaac's mother-in-law had left her daughter's room to help the cook with food for the next day.[9] While she was gone, the newborn suddenly disappeared from the cradle, and for the next two hours, people speculated wildly. Some blamed the Gypsy women who'd been roaming near the house for several days, and some neighbors investigated and made complaints to the mayor. Then around half an hour before my grandfather's arrival, while bringing some broth to Isaac's wife, someone noticed the bedroom window partly open and found the child—freezing cold, all blue and bruised but fortunately still alive—lying at his mother's feet.

"My grandfather slapped his forehead.

"'Tell me, Isaac, what time did your son disappear?'

"'Between nine and eleven.'

"'When was he found?'

"'Just after eleven thirty.'

---

[9] Meal celebrating the *bris mileh* (circumcision).

"'Isaac, are you sure you didn't skip anything that must be done in a Jewish home when a mother is in childbed?'

"'Almost sure.'

"'You had the rabbi say prayers?'

"'The rabbi of Herrlisheim is still here, in the next room, saying the usual prayers for the eve of a *bris mileh*.'

"'Who is looking after the new mother?'

"'Hendel, my mother-in-law, right here.'

"'Hendel,' said my grandfather, 'Have Psalms been placed in the room with the mother and child?'

"'Of course!' exclaimed Hendel.

"'You're sure they're not corrupted?'[10]

"'The Hebrew bookseller I bought them from hung them on the wall himself.'

"'Are your *mezuzahs* in order?'

"'I had new ones attached to every doorway.'

"Grandfather couldn't imagine what had gone wrong... But suddenly an idea struck him.

"'Hendel,' he said again, 'did you do the *circles* ceremony?'[11]

"In response, Hendel fainted. She had forgotten.

"'You know, your child is still alive thanks to me,' said my grandfather.

---

[10] Psalms are said to be *pusel* (corrupted) when they contain omissions or nonstandard spelling, or when the paper is torn or damaged.

[11] This ceremony involves using a sword, knife or other sharp implement to trace several circles around the head of the new mother and the newborn, to exorcise any malign influence and keep evil spirits away. Normally, a close relative performs this process, which must be repeated every evening at dusk throughout the mother's confinement.

"And he explained what had happened behind the white wall, in the little meadow."

"Now that's what I call a story, Samuel!" said Papa Salomon.

"Wait for the ending," replied the inexhaustible storyteller. "Ah, you thought it was over? Grandfather had gotten off easy for someone traveling on a Saturday evening. Naturally, the good people whose child he'd saved were quick to praise and pamper him. They asked him to stay the night. When he refused, they said they hoped he would at least stay for some food and drink, but he was no glutton just as he was no coward. Grandfather was back on the road scarcely half an hour after arriving.

"The dangerous time of night had passed[12] but my grandfather felt uneasy when he saw that white wall again. Crossing the meadow, he found nothing but a few locks of hair and some crushed eggshells on the snow. He was rounding the corner of the wall when suddenly, something furry tangled itself between his legs and rubbed against him. It was a big black cat that curled and uncurled its tail and kept meowing in a whimpering, pleading tone.

"'Perhaps one of the creatures I saw earlier?' thought my grandfather, and he reached into his pocket for his *tefillin*.

"Oh, no! He'd left them on the table when he took off his cloak at Isaac's. The big cat stood before him. It began meowing plaintively again and proffered a paw, which

---

[12] The critical time is the hour before midnight.

seemed to point to a nearby tree in which some clothes were fluttering. Grandfather understood.

"'She's one of the group from earlier,' he told himself. 'Her memory must be failing. She probably forgot her *shemmes*[13] and how to transform herself and retrieve her skirts. I won't be the one to return them.'

"Then he said loudly, '*Earthly or unearthly?*'[14]

"The cat meowed. Then grandfather brandished his stick, raised his arm in the air and struck the cat so hard he broke one of her front paws. The cat yowled and vanished.

"Grandfather walked so fast that it was barely daylight when he reached Bollwiller.

"'My wife,' he told himself, 'may still be asleep. Since I'm up, I'll take my hundred-sous coin and buy a sack of potatoes from old Mey.'

"He turned up the little street on the corner and found Mey's door wide open. Grandfather entered the courtyard and walked past the press and into the shed. When he reached the kitchen doorway, he called out. No one replied, so he entered the kitchen. That normally tidy room was a shambles: brooms strewn about, and near the hearth, broken plates and a little freshly fallen soot.

"A groaning sound came from the bedroom.

"'Hello? Neighbor Mey!! I've been calling to you for an hour.'

---

[13] Kabbalistic numbers that help sorcerers and sorceresses work their marvels.

[14] *Geheuer oder ungeheuer* in German. Anyone encountering a questionable creature in the night must, before acting, utter this standard phrase.

"Old Mey bid him enter. She was in bed.

"'Yudel,' she said, 'I'll give you some potatoes for free, but do me one favor. You're a good man, I know that.'

"'What's wrong?'

"'Oh, I'm in such pain!'

"'Did you fall while doing your work before dawn?'

"'Ow! Yes, there was work before dawn but it was dirty work: I was carried off, you see, and since the door was locked, I had to get back in a different way...'

"'Oh! Oh, were you making a neighborly visit to little Mr. Seppi and your husband got jealous and beat you?'

"'Ow! It wasn't him. He's been at the fair for three days.'

"'Then who was it?'

"'You won't reveal my secret?'

"'No! Who hurt you?'

"'It was you.'

"'And when could I have injured you?'

"'This morning.'

"'This morning! What time?'

"'Between one and two o'clock.'

"'Clearly you've lost your mind. At one in the morning, I was eight leagues from here.'

"'Yes, but when you hurt me...' she said, and she showed him her left arm, which was in a sling.

"'Well?'

"'It wasn't my arm then, but... you know... the black cat's paw? I'd asked you for my clothing but you refused to understand. Go, Yudel, and fetch my skirts before my husband returns. They're in the tree near the stone bridge...'

"My grandfather yelped and escaped as fast as his legs could go. He told no one of that adventure as long as the *other* lived. As for me, I'm sure it's all true, since my grandfather wasn't a liar."

Samuel stood up.

"Samuel," said the master of the house, "you can boast that you've given us an excellent Friday evening."

Just then the cuckoo clock in the corner struck ten. My host sprang to his feet.

"My dear friend," he said to me, "it's time to rest. You must be tired. The *Shabbes goye* will light the way and show you to your room."

Turning to Samuel, he added half-joking and half-seriously, "You and your tales of sorcery may keep me awake tonight. They always stick in the brain and cause bad dreams. Oh, and in case I don't see you before then, remember to stop by on Tuesday morning at ten to trim my beard before we leave for the wedding."

Samuel nodded, wished us "*Gut Shabbes*, everyone!" and left humming a melody that would be chanted the next morning in synagogue.

I did have trouble sleeping but not quite for the reasons that seemed to trouble Papa Salomon. First, my mind kept distracting me with images of all the physical and spiritual pleasures awaiting me at Yekel's son's wedding. Then I was kept up by a noise that had been coming from the next room for about a quarter of an hour. It sounded like a lively dispute among the usually close-knit brothers. I hasten to add that I found out the nature and cause of that spirited argument when the end of a com-

ment floated through the partition wall. The voice be-
longed, I think, to the eldest son.

"I tell you, we can't leave the hall door open like that.
And since you're all too chicken-hearted to go down, I'll
go myself. *I'm* not afraid of any black cat."

After that, I heard nothing but a heavy tread on the
stair and what sounded like a man's voice singing.

I suppose our brave hero was trying to pluck up his
courage, like Sosie.[15]

The next day, we all arose early for synagogue. After
morning services and dinner (they dine at midday), I
went to visit some family and friends of my host. He of
course accompanied me on these rounds, as did his wife.
With his hands held just below his chest, plunged beatifi-
cally into the long sleeves of his blue frock coat, Papa
Salomon walked us down through the village at that slow,
solemn pace that a rural Jew affects particularly on the
Sabbath and holy days. Our first visit was to Uncle Yekel.
The jovial young men of the village were gathered at his
house, noisily celebrating the *Spinholtz*. That is a kind of
party the groom throws for his comrades on the last Saturday afternoon before his marriage. It is like a farewell
to his boyhood. The bride does the same for her friends,
and surely at that moment in Wintzenheim, the daughter
of the honorable *parness* was offering similar hospitality
to the young women of her village.

Uncle Yekel, as my host had predicted, invited me to
the wedding and insisted on it in the most cordial man-

---

[15] Translator's note: A character in Molière's comedy *Amphitryon*.

ner. I would not have refused anyway, and we spent the rest of the day visiting various neighbors.

On our return, we found some twenty people settled in at Papa Salomon's, chatting boisterously while glancing out the window every so often to see if the evening star had appeared in the sky. These faithful souls were in the habit of coming over in winter—sometimes on Fridays, always on Saturdays—to pray together at Papa Salomon's.[16] In our villages, this is considered an honor for the host, accorded only to men who, like my friend, are well respected in the *kehillah*.[17]

The final words of their evening prayers had the same effect as the whistle that sounds in a theater to signal a scene change. Sabbath was over. Instantly, the room took on a new look: tablecloths disappeared and the seven-spouted lamp was hoisted to the black wooden ceiling. Then six or seven men entered, each with a cotton cap on his head, a freshly lit pipe in his mouth and a lantern in hand. Their custom in winter was to spend Saturday evening playing cards at the Salomon home. The victor would take home not cash but an in-kind prize. For that quarter of an hour, it consisted of a plump snow-white goose hanging proudly from a window hook, awaiting its fortunate owner. You should have seen the lucky winner stand suddenly and dispatch a messenger to his wife, announcing he had won *it*! You might have mistaken the

---

[16] A gathering of ten people over the age of thirteen is enough to form a congregation of the faithful. [Translator's note: In the orthodox tradition, specifically ten men.]

[17] Congregation or community.

scene for one of those indoor tableaux captured so admirably by master painters of the Flemish school. Nothing was missing to complete the illusion: not the rustically simple room and furniture, not the genial profiles, not the tankards of beer within the players' reach, not the puffs of tobacco smoke. Now add a fat yellow tomcat forced to witness all these indoor scenes, crouched cozily behind the stove, its back arched, its tail up, watching our players with that placid look of deep observation that cats have taken on ever since Hoffmann proved to them that they had philosophers in their ancestry.

"Rabbi, is this goose *kosher*?"

CHAPTER THREE

Travel preparations. — A secular digression cut short. — Conversation. — An entire community. — Marem, the parness. — A sick child. — Arrival. — Eve of the wedding. — A guest room. — The village watchman.

MY HOST'S NEPHEW WAS to marry on the next Wednesday. This meant traveling to Wintzenheim, a village seven leagues from Bollwiller, for the celebration. Papa Salomon took me there along with his elder and younger daughters.

Salomon and his brother considered it safer, more convenient and more comfortable to go by private carriage than to be shut up in a railroad car. So the previous evening, they had hired two vehicles of the kind that country folk pretentiously call *chars-à-bancs*—chariots with benches—though their seats have more plank than *banc* about them. One carriage was for the groom and his family and the other for the Salomons. Our group was finally ready to leave around ten in the morning, but the master of the house had not yet come down. While waiting, we climbed into our seats. Papa Salomon appeared at last on the upstairs landing, talking with someone we could not see. Judging from his head and hand movements, he was expressing pure satisfaction to the other person. Then Salomon came down, nimble and sprightly for a seventy-year-old. His light-brown Garrick coat with a thousand cape collars covered his shoulders. His cotton cap was pulled down over his ears, with a round hat planted on top. He delightedly coaxed thick puffs of smoke from a beautiful meerschaum pipe with a decorative lid and silver chain, filled with so-called *violet* tobacco, whose aroma of contraband you could smell at ten paces. This pipe and this tobacco were for special occasions only. Taking his place next to us, he smiled at me contentedly as if to ask, "What? Nothing to say? Don't you admire me?"

On closer inspection of Papa Salomon's chin, I easily noticed the handiwork of the barber–storyteller. Samuel had just finished shaving my companion with a skill that would have made Figaro proud, even though Samuel did not have access to a Bilbao razor but only humble scissors from Bouxwiller: the only kind of tool that Jewish law lets travel over orthodox beards.[1] I therefore understood Papa Salomon's legitimate satisfaction. Though he had obeyed the religious prescription, his beard was no less well groomed; he relished the pleasure of overcoming the difficulty.

Thanks to our obliging horses and the dry weather of that fine November morning, we made outstanding time on the winding route along the foot of the Vosges. Crossing

---

[1] "Ye shall not cut round the corners of the hair of your head, neither shalt thou destroy the corners of thy beard" (Leviticus, 19:27). Based on this commandment, the Talmud banned the use of razors, for they destroy quickly. Scissors are tolerated, though, probably because they work more slowly. It is a casuistic interpretation and yet the faithful abide by it.

A Jewish barber.

one of the prettiest valleys in Upper Alsace, so rich in memories and historic monuments, any traveler on a less urgent schedule would surely have let his imagination roam. Such a traveler would have taken excursions into the past, if only in thought. The setting was beautiful: At right, appealing hillocks and gorges punctuated an open plain that recalled the Thirty Years' War, part of which was fought here. The landscape echoed the names of the great men of that fight. At left, ruined fortresses were perched sporadically like eagles' nests on the mountaintops of the Vosges, half-bathed in morning mist, evoking other eras and ways of life. They spoke of the Middle Ages and feudalism, Crusades and tournaments, bells ringing in towers and the cry of hunting horns, ladies imprisoned in dungeons, helmeted knights-errant clad in iron, each with a lance at his side and a falcon on his fist, galloping over the heath on a faithful steed to rescue the damsel of his dreams.

As for me, I took care not to slide down that slope. I was on this journey largely to gather direct impressions of the simple, rustic life of country Jews, and I did not wish to deviate from my plan. To cut temptation short, I hurried my traveling companion into a conversation that would lead me straight to that goal.

"Tell me, Papa Salomon! Are there still as many Jewish villagers in Wintzenheim as there once were? As you know, I used to go there quite often and knew the place well, but that was fifteen years ago. It must be very different now. I'll be a total stranger there! So tell me a little about what the *kehillah* (community) is like these days."

Once I sent him in that direction, Papa Salomon unleashed his old man's loquacity and went into detail about things I already knew in part. The village of Wintzenheim has many Jewish residents and enjoys all the advantages of a large community. There is a beautifully built synagogue, a Jewish community school, a chief rabbinate and numerous *chevres* (societies). Wintzenheim's prayer leader is, as Papa Salomon put it, nothing short of a celebrity *hazzan* who would be worthy of singing at the central synagogue in Frankfurt. The happy *parness* (president) of that blessed community was Marem, whose daughter's wedding we were to attend. Marem earned a very comfortable living selling wine lees and goatskins, which let him give his eldest daughter a dowry of three thousand pounds in hard cash and a trousseau besides, even though he still had two other daughters to marry off. Loved and esteemed by the whole village, by Catholics and Jews alike, Marem would have been the luckiest man in the world if God had not cruelly tested his paternal affections: for three years, his youngest child, his only son, had been wasting away from consumption, that dread disease so tragically common in Alsace.

"In other words," I said, "this won't be a very festive wedding, will it?"

"You might think not," replied Salomon, "but these poor people are used to living with their misfortune. They no longer see its severity. And they rightly hope in God's goodness, for God is all powerful and is the *shomer Yisroel* (guardian of Israel). Anyway, the people of Wintzenheim, you'll recall, know how to celebrate. You'll see. All in all, it will be great fun."

The time flew and before I knew it, the village of Wintzenheim appeared.

Our drivers made a brief halt. They put decorative red ribbons on their hats and on their little horses' manes and tails. Then they sat tall in their seats, cracked whips and sped us to the Marem house through a long line of onlookers. The *parness* gave us a welcome that mirrored his ancestors' traditional hospitality in Palestine. Indeed, we might have believed we were in the ancient Near East if not for the sharp November cold and, in particular, the cotton cap on the head of our respectable host.

That supper made me anticipate the wedding feast even more. Salomon's nephew, seated next to his fiancée, took a jewel case from his long frock coat. He opened it and placed it in front of her, revealing several pieces of jewelry. Bridegrooms always give brides these types of gifts on the night before the wedding, the evening of *sablonoth*, which is Hebrew for "presents." Every prominent Jew in the village came to see the Marems and their guests, and the crowd talked noisily. Only the lady of the house stayed painfully silent. Her hands were intertwined tenderly with the emaciated fingers of a kind of ghost with red, jutting cheeks, hollow eyes and a harsh cough, who sat near her in a rolling armchair. I recognized him as the poor consumptive child that Salomon had mentioned.

We went to bed around eleven. The Marems' home was not vast enough for all the overnight guests, so sev-

eral of us stayed with neighbors. That aspect of local
manners deserves a brief mention. What if an Alsatian
villager is entertaining more company than he can house?
No need to knock at the inn. Every affluent Jewish home-
owner has a guest room somewhere in the house, not just
for his own visitors but also for friends' guests. So I slept
at the home of a nearby friend. The room I was led to was
almost a model of the genre: four whitewashed walls decorated with all manner of colored engravings, a walnut
chest of drawers with brass handles, and sitting on a large
cabinet as if for decoration, a range of admirably pre-
served pears and apples of the most luscious varieties. In
one corner, above a faience stove, a green étagère held
two painted plaster rabbits whose heads bobbed with
pendulum-like regularity thanks to an unseen weight and
counterweight. In another corner, a fir-wood frame supported a bed whose prodigious height came from five or
six mattresses and two or three straw pallets, plus an un-
derlying layer of bundled vines. Around the bed hung a
scarlet-trimmed white muslin curtain that opened and
closed on a circular rod fixed to the ceiling. Despite fatigue from the day's journey, I stayed up a while longer to
examine the plain, rustic items in my guest room, which
reminded me of my childhood. But suddenly and by a
curious means, I was warned that it was getting late and
it was time for bed. From the far side of the hamlet, I
seemed to hear the voice of the *veilleur*—the night
watchman—announcing the hour. This is common practice in the Alsatian countryside. Only the methods vary
by local custom and tradition.

In villages in Upper Alsace, travelers sleeping on the ground floor of an inn on a main street are often startled awake by vigorous cracks of a whip wielded by an expert hand. The number of cracks tells you the hour.

In villages near the banks of the Rhine, you know the time by the number of raspy sounds someone coaxes from a long reed-pipe, accompanied by plaintive howling of nearby dogs. For the uninitiated, nothing is more sinister and jarring than this bizarre clock.

To give Wintzenheim its due, I must say they announce the time in a much more civilized way. No whips or reed-pipes for them: just a human voice that tells you the hour very politely, in rhymed prose no less.

I heard the watchman's solid footsteps in the street, the thud of his shoes alternating with the clang of his iron-tipped pike on the pavement. As he approached, I could make out his refrain more clearly. He halted just under my window and then, with a remarkable bass voice —slightly nasal and very rhythmic—he repeated this simple quatrain in German patois:

Horiche vos i aych vel zoye:
Di glok het zvelfi gshloye
Bevore fir ond licht
Dos u ole Got behit.[2]

---

[2] Translation:
"Listen to what I will tell you:
The bell has struck midnight.
Extinguish your fire and your light,
So God will watch over us all."

I immediately stacked chairs on chairs in order to climb and storm that Homeric bed, and I hurriedly blew out my candle, obeying the watchman's wise advice.

CHAPTER FOUR

Wintzenheim. — The wedding: first ceremony of the morning; tithe distribution; the tressing ceremony; the great procession; a sacred melody; the wedding benediction; the broken bottle; gifts; a full band; groomsmen and bridesmaids; the dance hall. — Digression, the venue and its seasonal transformations: fencing hall in spring, granary in summer, theater in winter: puppets; Maestro Rodolphe; his dual-purpose repertoire; announcements; the audience, the character of Hans Wurst. — Back on topic: the dance and the dancers; affordable refreshments; a consoling maxim.

THE NEXT DAY, I rose early though I had stayed up extremely late. Before joining the other guests at the Marems', I wanted to tour this village that I had visited so frequently as a child. Now I explored it with pure, indescribable joy. This quaint, alluring community was built at the mouth of one of the loveliest Alsatian valleys, the Munster Valley. It stands at the very foot of the Haut-Landsberg mountain, which is thick with black fir trees and crowned by an old castle.[1] Try to picture the curiously constructed homes: some with pointed gables and

---

[1] Haut-Landsberg castle was built and fortified, they say, by the house of Hohenstauffen.

carved wooden fronts, others with protruding bay or oriel windows. See that small public square planted with acacias, cooled constantly by the large fountain whose stone basin, fed by six brass pipes, serves as a watering place for cattle. Summer, however, is when Wintzenheim is at its most idyllically enchanting. Each morning at the same hour, you can watch oxen and heifers come mooing out of their barns when a herdsman calls to them on a crude reed-pipe and leads them to the communal pasture. In summer, you can eagerly inhale the strong, fresh scent of the hills and orchards that surround the area, spreading their perfume everywhere. A delectable breeze from the valley sweeps through the main street while two stripes of clear water, diverted from the Fecht,[2] run parallel on either side for the length of the village before merging again just beyond its limits and disappearing into the winding, fertile grasslands. Then the pretty peasant girls of the valley, nimble and short-skirted, drive donkeys before them laden with baskets of vegetables, butter and fresh eggs. They come to sell them to the Jewish mothers who sit on large wooden beams, busily babbling and knitting.

Despite the intense cold, the village was unusually animated that day. Men and women came and went, lighthearted and bustling. During our country weddings, everybody tries hard to make things pleasant, as if it were their personal responsibility.

---

[2] A stream that flows from the Vosges into the Ill, a tributary of the Rhine.

People wake up very early on a wedding day and make the inside of each home especially tidy. They also put effort into their personal appearance. The reason is simple: weddings attract visitors from other places; these visitors might have sons and daughters; those sons and daughters might be of marrying age; a match might be made. Parents, boys and girls all have an incentive to make a good impression.

The bridegroom, accompanied by close friends or relatives, enters the synagogue early to pray. Around eight o'clock he goes out to meet his bride, who is brought to the building's peristyle. In the shade of the roofed walkway, the couple is asked to sit on a bench with a backrest, made of mahogany that is covered in Hebrew inscriptions. The rabbi then spreads a white cloth *(tallith)* over their heads and everyone scatters handful after handful of rye and wheat onto the cloth as a symbol of fertility. Given the size of Jewish families, though, we can say without fear of being called impious that this ritual is practically redundant.

When I returned to the Marem house, the courtyard was full and tumultuous. A chaotic, noisy crowd buzzed, squeezing impatiently around a table placed in the middle of the space. This table held piles of coins totaling some 250 francs. A man, presumably a friend of the family, was there urging all the guests to state their name and connection to the couple. It was a proper Babel of garb, languages and shouting. Men in tunics and caps spoke the local patois wonderfully; these were the natives. Another group had round hats and wore threadbare frock coats decorated with steel-blue buttons. They carried chestnut walking sticks topped with orange wool that was laced with brass wire, and spoke a German that was a bit less incorrect, though still very queer; these were neighbors from across the Rhine, in Germany. Still others, with angular features, high foreheads and square shoulders, wore broad-brimmed headgear that failed to hide thick curls of black hair. Their most distinctive garments were a caftan of unidentifiable color and turned-down boots that had once been waxed with egg; they pronounced *u* distinctly like an *i* and were subjects of His Imperial Majesty, the Autocrat of all the Russias. These were all indigent Jews. Every last one—Alsatians, Germans, Poles—lived on the charity of their brethren. Every Friday evening, in a rare spirit of solidarity, some fellow Jew was sure to give them a good meal and a place to sleep in exchange for a housing voucher called a *blet*. This ticket is issued to indigent Jews as they enter any borough inhabited by their coreligionists. The head of any family, however humble, deems it a pleasure and duty to take his turn hosting a disinherited fellow Jew at his table—"under his lamp," as we say. The idea is that on the day of rest, this warm family hospitality might help the destitute forget the trials of their wandering life. Today that whole vagabond population gathered in one spot, attracted of course by the wedding. By ancient custom, they had come for their share of the tithe. This generous tradition has survived among us across the centuries, especially among country Jews! The simplest rural Jewish weddings might involve a dowry of just five hundred

Distribution of the tithe.

francs, but a tenth of that modest sum will invariably pass into the hands of the needy.

As I pondered this pious distribution, I saw almost a dozen matrons push their way through the throng and enter the house with a purposeful look on their faces. Their rather dated clothes suggested that I was looking at the *doyennes* of the area, who surely knew all the local ways and practices for such solemn days. I suspected they were about to perform some ancient rite that men were forbidden to witness. So I sneaked after them into a small room off the parlor and squatted stealthily behind the door, hiding as best I could behind an old folding screen with small openings in it, placed by chance within my reach. This transparent rampart let me see everything without being seen. At the center of the room sat the bride, emotional and pale. Her beautiful black maidenly hair fell in curls over her shoulders—for the final time, alas! Gathered close around her, numerous women whispered. When the matrons entered, everyone stood. The matrons crossed the room decisively, approached the girl and handed out combs. With all the fervor of a religious act, this female assemblage immediately surrounded the poor bride. In holy resignation, she let them grab at her hair, distribute it haphazardly, separate it into tresses, roll them up quickly and stuff them unceremoniously under a small black satin cap that would hide them forever. Jews give special importance to hair as one of a woman's most beautiful ornaments, and on entering married life she must sacrifice it to her husband. For his sake, she must renounce all desire to appear attractive and must willingly forego all allure.

I am honestly not too sure that this law always achieves its aim: often, the young wife's charms are only heightened by the pretty little cap with pink and blue ribbons that sits over the black satin cap, or by the velvet band meant to replace her hair. This band and especially the wigs that were devised later violate the older tradition, which stringently allowed only a simple lace covering in place of hair. The lace fell over a pretty, pale forehead, creating a certain entrancing air of modesty and chastity.

Such was the *tressing* ceremony. When the bride returned to the courtyard, the procession formed to go to synagogue for the wedding benediction. Six musicians led the way. Next came the bride, veiled and clothed in her mortuary garments (as is customary), wearing a kind of turban with thin gold strips, leaning on the arms of her mother and her future mother-in-law. Beside and behind her—in order of kinship, importance or intimacy—walked the matrons of Wintzenheim and the neighboring villages, stiff and starched in their ceremonial regalia, sparkling with jewelry and precious stones. Jewish women have a passion for jewelry that seems to have come down to them from the East. Though they no longer wear bells on their neck or rings in their nose (as in Isaiah's time), they now have rings on their fingers and chains on their shoulders. Even the poorest Jewish country women have a small trove of jewels that are the apple of their eye. I know more than one who, pressed by need, would go without food for a week rather than part with her small jewelry box, kept carefully since the *sablonoth* evening of her wedding.

Behind these women came the bridegroom. On his right walked his father Yekel and Uncle Salomon, and on his left, his father-in-law, who was the honest *parness* of the village. Next came a great many strangers. Here and there among the young men were aged grandfathers from another era, whose clothes evoked old courtly fashions: men's brick-red or apple-green *grands habits* with long basques, short velvet breeches, striped blue cotton stockings, a waistcoat with a floral design, buckle shoes and a three-cornered hat. They looked like the last representatives of Jewish Alsace before 1789.[3] Right on time, the procession set out and walked past a long line of curious neighbors of every faith. It paraded through the village as clarinets sentimentally played the well-known *chuppah*[4] song—a heart-rending, crudely elegiac melody that, for perhaps the hundredth time in my life, moved me to tears.

Under the *chuppah* (canopy) in the midst of the synagogue, the venerable rabbi awaited the betrothed couple. After the usual prayer, he blessed a cup of wine and presented it to them and they drank from it. The bridegroom then took a large ring from his finger and slipped it onto his young bride's hand, saying these sacramental words: "With this ring, be consecrated unto me according to the

---

[3] Translator's note: The French Revolution began in 1789. These old men wear fashions dating from France's monarchic era.

[4] Or *wedding canopy*. It is under this canopy (*chuppah* in Hebrew) that the blessing is given.

Law of Moses and of Israel." The rabbi recited another
prayer and they left amid shouts of congratulations. The
serious, solemn part of the wedding was over. The emotional faces brightened and the music roused us. After
the melancholy *chuppah* song came a joyous, hurried
march. Jews, however, are always reminded to temper our
joy. On our way back through the village, not far from the
synagogue, I noticed someone apparently waiting for the
procession: a little man swinging a bottle in his hands.
Just as we passed, he smashed the full bottle of wine
against a wall, covering the street with its debris. The little man was none other than the *shammes* (the
synagogue's beadle) and by simple allegory, the broken
bottle reminded us of how fragile things are here below.
Tragically, that very day I would realize how close together grief and happiness can be.

The newlyweds, who had been fasting until then, went
back to the Marem house for breakfast. All the guests
were there. Though it was daytime, six tallow candles
burned in a corner of the room on a small table that held
two bags bulging with cash. Two people, who by tradition
must not be relatives or friends of the household, each
unsealed one bag and counted the contents by candlelight. A few minutes later, thirty stacks of one hundred
francs each, the whole dowry, had been spread out in full
view in beautiful hundred-sous coins. Honor was declared
satisfied. Across the room at a square table, the village
hazzan (prayer leader) sat gravely with a pen in hand and
a register book before him. He wore ceremonial garb: a
black velvet skullcap, a white cravat, and huge false to-

pazes on both his chest and his little fingers. Anyone bearing a wedding gift for the young couple walked up to this table and the *hazzan* registered it, announcing loudly and clearly the object given and the name of the giver. Each item elicited cries of surprise and admiration. I had already heard announcements of a seven-spouted copper oil lamp, a fountain with two spouts, four dozen pewter plates, a pair of candlesticks with snuffers, sixty yards of cloth, a spinning wheel, an oil cruet, six pairs of bedsheets and a complete collection of prayer books for all the festivals (Soultzbach edition), when the *hazzan*'s voice was overpowered by a clarinet tuning up: the signal for dancing. In Alsatian villages, wedding guests dance by day and feast by night, and have no less fun as a result.

Groomsmen and maids of honor arrived soon, radiant with joy, each boy escorting two girls. Some relatives stayed with the sick child, who was tired from the day's activities. They would rejoin us a bit later. The masters of ceremonies were the night watchman and his friend the *garde-champêtre* (a combination fieldkeeper and rural policeman), each holding a beribboned pike in one hand and a jug of wine for the musicians in the other. The band consisted of a hunting horn, two clarinets, a serpent, two trombones and a big drum. The drummer, unable to make himself heard so far, was ready for vengeance: he attacked the donkey skin so energetically that he made the windows shake. In Alsace, everyone knows that a village party is hardly worth attending unless there is a big drum.

To reach the dance, you had to travel almost to the middle of the fields. Let me describe the changes that this room underwent for different events.

In spring, it was a fencing hall.

In summer, at harvest time, the owner piled his sheaves of wheat there and rats and mice swarmed through the place.

In winter, it was the theater. Late each autumn, as the north winds started to blow and the fogs of Haut-Landsberg settled over the village, and as distressed titmice sought refuge in the shingle traps in the bare treetops, from October 15 to 20 on the road from Colmar to Wintzenheim, you were sure to find a long, enclosed wagon painted green, drawn by two worn-out horses. Resting peacefully in this wagon, entwined in a thick network of strings, was a whole population of wooden figurines depicting kings, queens, madonnas, devils as black as sin, long-bearded hermits and so on. The arrival of Maestro Rodolphe, director of this marionette company, was like a festival in Wintzenheim. He was a locksmith during the off season (summer), but when the rain and the cold came, Maestro Rodolphe traded the mechanical arts for the liberal arts. An imposing presence, he always knew what to say to make people laugh. At precisely two o'clock on the day of a big performance, you should have seen him in his Napoleonic costume, riding through the village on his nag preceded by a mirthful troop of children. His trumpet would bring out an inquisitive flock in cotton caps and wooden shoes. Maestro Rodolphe gave them a detailed account of the day's show. On Sundays, our performer entertained a Catholic public: from atop his slow-moving wagon, he would announce a drama about the life of poor Genevieve of Brabant or some episode from the lives of the saints and martyrs. On Friday evenings, though, he played to followers of another faith: Maestro Rodolphe portrayed the adventure of Joseph, so wickedly sold by his brothers, or the heroism of Judith or the mercy of King Ahasuerus. To complete the illusion and heighten the local color, Maestro Rodolphe made sure to announce that beautiful Esther and her uncle Mordecai would express themselves in "Hebrew." By this he meant they would speak the Judeo-German patois used in Alsace. Maestro Rodolphe seemed to think that *Yiddish* was once the official language of the Courts of Shushan and Babylon.

How the spectators admired the sober, stiff gait of those wooden puppets! How everyone listened to those bombastic tirades spoken in voices that were now deep, now nasal, now falsetto! Then came the highlight, when the audience's attention increased and their hearts were in their ears and eyes. That happened when an astounding volley of swearing and a ribald song announced the arrival of a hunched figure—practically doubled over, arms dangling, head tilted maliciously, eye winking and teeth clattering. This was the main attraction, the comic figure, the reluctant hero of the piece, *Hans Wurst*.[5] Like the characters in ancient Atellan farces, whose direct

---

[5] "John Sausage." This character was already celebrated in Viennese theater long ago. (See Lessing's *Dramaturgie de Hambourg*.)

descendant he seems to be, Hans Wurst often stopped to rebuke some weak joker in the crowd who had dared to provoke him, and who might have gotten away with such impishness elsewhere. Hans Wurst, who had a glib tongue and knew his public, replied with taunts and jeers that turned the audience's laughter against the hapless troublemaker. Sometimes even unprovoked—and frankly, for the sheer pleasure of being mean—Hans Wurst's dialogue with fellow marionettes included thinly veiled references to recent events. Pity anyone who had wronged Maestro Rodolphe in any way during his stay in Wintzenheim! His invincible clown would take revenge. He was no more sparing of the Catholic world than the Jewish world, of church sextons than synagogue *hazzans*, of the niece of a priest than the son of a rabbi, of the great than the small, of the city dweller than the villager. Rampant vice, fashionable foolishness, passing scandals—all were fair game for him. Raising his hoarse voice mockingly, he named specific people and things with Aristophanic license, and emphasized his words with frantic gestures. Hans Wurst was the joy of gossips and the terror of bad consciences.

These performances occurred in the same space where we recently left the Marem wedding ball. Turning the theater into a ballroom was easy. The white walls had no decorative hangings other than old cobwebs. The ventilation was a bit too good, as wind whistled through four windows that were missing their glass despite the bitter weather. Merry Jewish girls crowded along the walls. They wore aprons of shot silk and bright dresses short enough to show off the wide black moire ribbons down their stockings as they danced. On their feet they wore calfskin shoes shaped like the head of a pike fish, which have been popular in the region since time immemorial. The couple's parents and both families' friends and guests soon yielded to the musicians' call. Then the bride and bridegroom appeared. She wore her wedding afternoon clothes: a luminous silk dress, a lace mantelet, and a cap brimming with pink ribbons.

Meanwhile, the big drum boomed, the trombones' slides moved in and out, the clarinets whistled. People do not dance the polka here or the redowa or the mazurka, but rather the three-beat waltz, the loveliest of all dances. They have such fun at celebrations that they never think to cool off with refreshments. Usually the girls are content to take off their shoulder scarves and the boys their waistcoats. After each waltz, the watchman and the *garde-champêtre* go around the room, each with a large watering-pot, and sprinkle water indiscriminately on the parquet floor, the onlookers and the dancers.

The sun began to set. Suddenly, I felt two taps on my shoulder. I wheeled around and found myself looking into the smiling face of Papa Salomon.

"I hope," he said, "you do not regret coming with us from Bollwiller to Wintzenheim?"

"Certainly not."

"Well, listen. It's getting dark and some of the guests are already slipping out. So follow me."

"But where?" I asked, still entranced by the spectacle of the dancing.

"What do you mean 'where'? To the wedding banquet, by Heaven! I don't want to be one of the last to arrive. For both our sakes, I want to get a good spot."

Since I was still hesitating, Papa Salomon's tone shifted from playful to sententious:

"Young man," he said to me, "everything in its time. There is a time to dance but there is also a time to eat."

I thought it a fine philosophy, very consoling if not original. So I followed good Papa Salomon.

A tempting kugel.

CHAPTER FIVE

Raphael and Leah. — The wedding banquet; two inevitable dishes. — A gallery of village types: the hazzan and assistant hazzans, the schoolmaster, the amateur lustik, the paid lustik, the shammes. — A sad interruption.

AT THE EDGE of the village, at the end of a narrow lane, a simple dwelling has been occupied for nearly half a century by Raphael and his worthy companion, Leah. It is the finest restaurant in the area, and people say a wedding dinner is not a wedding dinner unless it is cooked by Leah and served by Raphael, who is his wife's head waiter.

That evening, an unusual flood of light poured out through the round windows of the small house. It was lit not just by wall candles but also a whole series of seven-spouted oil lamps hanging over a long, narrow table and a dazzling white tablecloth with broad red stripes. The reception was in the dining room, as always. The only people missing were the young bride and her family. They had been delayed, we soon learned, because the poor sick child was having an alarming attack. When they arrived at the banquet, the women gathered on one side and the men on the other in the time-honored way.

Food was served in the old style, one dish after another. But such dishes! Need I say that it was a very lengthy dinner? Just as it was winding down, reinforcements showed up: a new group of guests of both sexes. Everyone packed in tighter, and to occupy less space the men took off their frock coats. They also removed their hats and replaced them with their cotton caps. In our villages, when a family is invited as a group, they do not take it literally. It is good etiquette to send one or at most two people to the meal, and the rest come only for dessert. The hosts return the favor and order a plentiful, delicious dessert to compensate the voluntary latecomers. Dessert is where Leah's talent, artistry and fertile imagination shine. What didn't she serve us that evening! Most of all, we admired the two inevitable dishes: One is a cake depicting an eel resting on a dense thicket of boxwood. To be honest, I have never figured out why Leah's meals should include, even in artistic imitation, a food so categorically banned from the Jewish table by the Laws of Moses. Perhaps Leah wished to use this innocent illusion to console her guests for being deprived of that forbidden dish? The other, less unorthodox dish is called *nougat du fiancé*: the bridegroom's nougat, decorated with flowers and with little glowing wax candles. It was Raphael's special mission to carry it into the room triumphantly. Holding it in front of his head, the good fellow sang a peculiar tune and danced some grotesque *ronds de jambe* and *entrechats*. He placed the much-desired nougat on the table only after executing numerous marches, countermarches, circuits and detours at a calculatedly leisurely pace.

The guests included certain figures who are almost mandatory at any Jewish wedding. They were all stock types among the curious population in which I found myself.

The fellow who hums a prelude and holds his knife ready to beat out the rhythm is the prayer leader or *hazzan*, whom we had seen listing the wedding gifts that morning. As paid entertainment, he will now sing the highlights of his liturgical repertoire. Standing behind him, each wearing a hat, are two assistant *hazzans*: a tenor and a bass. These three are the vocal orchestra of the synagogue, where instrumental music is prohibited. The *hazzan*, who receives a salary from the congregation, is an important person whose job is relatively lucrative. From his income, he must also pay his two vocal accompanists. These apprentices will assist prayer leaders in different communities until the happy day when, after long trials and a nomadic life, they reach the esteemed position of *hazzan* themselves. Free from musical duties during the week, his assistants practice various trades. To supplement their meager fees, they charge a more than moderate price to teach children basic writing and reading, or they compete with the local barber and apply those famous Bouxwiller-made scissors to the chins of fellow Jews.

The assistant *hazzans* also have other talents to augment their revenue. Does a wealthy resident want to celebrate an answered prayer or unexpected good luck by giving a new *Sefer* (sacred Pentateuch scroll) to the synagogue? The assistants stage the ceremony leading up to the donation. Using pasteboard cutouts covered in moss and flowers, they improvise a Mount Sinai surrounded by rocks and ravines. There, the *Sefer*—an object of veneration for the faithful—is displayed for several days.

Before *Sukkoth* (the Feast of Booths), these apprentices are often in charge of building and adding hangings and decorations to the open-air booths where all good Jews must sojourn for eight days with their family, in memory of the Israelites' wanderings in the desert. Despite all these jobs, our assistant *hazzans* are still constantly forced to live by their wits. As true artists, they spend more than they earn: gambling, their favorite passion, absorbs most of their profits. When their purse runs dry—when their fixed income is spent and their secondary revenue gone—they take it in stride and wait for the High Holidays in September. During those holy days, which last more than two weeks, the *hazzan* cannot do without his assistants any more than a carriage can do without wheels or a windmill without sails. The congregation impatiently expects wonders at High Holiday services, and the vocal orchestra will need countless rehearsals. Our apprentices choose that exact moment to pick an unreasonable quarrel with the *hazzan* to extort a better deal. They suddenly demand much higher fees and threaten to go on strike. The poor *hazzan* cries treason and alternately threatens and flatters them. The two sly fellows stand their ground. An uproar ensues in the village, with factions and cabals for and against. The *parness* (president of the congregation) gets involved and the synagogue's administration raises a fuss. Meetings are held, negotiations undertaken, and transactions are proposed, spurned and finally adopted. Mock-serious scenes and passions ensue, like something out of *Le Lutrin*.[1]

Opposite the *hazzan* and facing me at the banquet sat a somber, severe young man. Of all the guests, only he kept his frock coat on and his head uncovered. Only he affectedly insisted on speaking French. In that hubbub of boisterous, unliterary conversation, only he ventured some observations on science and letters, telling me that many ancient writers had been great geniuses and that among the moderns, he considered Voltaire their peer. As we spoke, his punctiliously formal grammar betrayed his identity. All doubt was banished: this was the head of Wintzenheim's Judaic community school. A Jewish schoolmaster plays an important role in large communities. For many families, he is—like Mentor in the *Odyssey* —a source of wisdom. Sententious and scholarly at heart, he is valued for the depth of his aphorisms and the variety of his quotations. He keeps up with the latest news, spreads it and comments on it. This, too, is appreciated. And thanks to his numerous contacts, he is also successful at brokering marriages.

Far from the schoolmaster and almost at the end of the table, a convivial red-headed man with fine, mischievous features sat squarely in his chair and held court: Seligmann, the life of every party. After drumming the table with two forks to call attention, he had already performed uncanny imitations of all the eccentric characters in and near the village. Already, after disappearing for a

---

[1] Translator's note: A seventeenth-century parody of heroic poems, written by the French poet Nicolas Boileau.

few moments, he had reappeared, transformed into a
Turk riding a baker's trough like a wagon. Then he had
taken each guest's name, no matter how bizarre, and had
found a rhyme for it that drew applause and laughter because it described the person so perfectly.

Seligmann was the amateur *lustik* (entertainer),[2] amus-
ing us free of charge for the mere pleasure of it. At
another end of the table sat another *lustik*: a paid one
that the hosts of such celebrations always brought in
from his home in the former capital of Alsace. This was
none other than little Leon, better known as Lobshe the
Jester.[3] He did many sleight-of-hand tricks, melted five-
franc coins like wax by candlelight and promptly restored
them, tied handkerchiefs and cravats into a thousand in-
extricable knots and palmed people's rings and watch
chains, which he then produced from other spectators'
shoes or pockets. He also acted some grotesque scenes in
which he replied to himself with untiring eloquence. It
was also he (pardon the omission) who on the morning of
the wedding had sung to the tearful couple a song called
the *Kalleh-Lid* (bride's song), whose melody and words
are movingly sad.[4]

As Lobshe gabbled and cavorted, he was watched by
an eminent figure seated to his right, who completes this
village gallery. This little man, about sixty years old with
bright, sunken eyes, wore a black silk cap on his head and

---

[2] Translator's note: A wedding entertainer. In this case, *lustik* is short
for *lustik-macher*, also known as a *batchn*.

[3] In German, *Possenmacher*.

[4] As we shall see, this song is also sung nostalgically in other circumstances.

a silver ring on the little finger of each hand. That person, already glimpsed above, is the *shammes*. He is in charge of keeping order in the synagogue, where he performs all kinds of tasks. On a wedding day, he is responsible for certain traditional functions such as breaking the bottle and calling people in to the feast. He plays a part in all ceremonies, sad or merry. The *shammes* is generally feared and respected, for he is reputed to have direct dealings with Heaven. Is death about to visit a family? At least three days in advance, the *shammes* is forewarned by omens: three days in advance in the dead of night, he alone notes the ominous screech of the owl, the plaintive howling of dogs, the mysterious creak of furniture; he alone hears the burial tools kept in his home begin to move. A *shammes* also has strange visions. The *shammes* of Wintzenheim will tell you how once at dusk, just hours after the death of venerable Rabbi Hirsch, he saw a celestial flame hover over the bald forehead of the deceased holy man while Kabbalistic symbols drew themselves on the walls. There is one time of year when a *shammes* is most likely to see and hear things that not all humans can. That season is in autumn just before the *Days of Awe*, when Jews go to synagogue at dawn—or even earlier, in the middle of the night—for prayer and acts of devotion in preparation for *Yom Kippur* (the Day of Atonement). For ten days, devout souls do penance, and both the dead and the living are said to be uneasy and restless. The *shammes* has ghoulish encounters in those solemn moments: With his black cloak on his back and his wooden hammer in hand, he travels through the si-

lent hamlet each night for nearly two weeks, three hours
after midnight, knocking at the doors of Jewish homes to
call the faithful to prayer. He walks and with almost every
step there is a new apparition. In one place he is followed
by a long line of white ghosts: unfortunate men who
probably died a violent death, for they hold out their
fleshless hands to the *shammes* as if begging him for a
proper Jewish burial. Further along, he is assailed by a
flock of white geese: suffering, transmogrified sinners
that whirl raucously around him, uttering pitiful cries.
They accompany the *shammes* until he is just paces from
the synagogue. There, as if driven back by the holiness of
the place, their wings suddenly become heavy, their
moans dissipate and they vanish into the ground, only to
reappear at the same time and place the next night and
the following nights.

It is the *shammes* who collects the last sigh of the dying and closes their eyes. It is he who, at the home of the
deceased, in a remote side room, keeps a lonely vigil over
the body by the light of a flickering funeral lamp. Because
the synagogue must not be left empty on the eve of *Yom
Kippur* once the religiously stirred crowd leaves, it is he
who stays until morning. There he sits on the sacred platform with a Bible in his hand, wearing his shroud.[5] He
prays all night, never frightened by the crackle of the
eternal lamp that hangs in front of the Holy Ark, or by
the strange noises around midnight, when the dead come
to address their prayers to the God of Israel.

---

[5] That evening and all the next day, religious married men wear the
same white tunic that they will wear in their grave.

Naphthali Hirsch (1750–1823), former chief rabbi
of Wintzenheim. Artist unknown.

The end of the banquet was interrupted by sad news. The rabbi had barely recited the seven wedding benedictions when someone came to tell the Marems that the young patient had taken a bad turn, a very bad turn. The parents hurried out, taking most of the guests with them.

At the cemetery.

CHAPTER SIX

Funeral and grief. — A historical explanation. — The house of mourning; prayers; the shroud; the funeral summons; the Mechilah; the procession; reconciliation; profaned water; the Angel of Death. — The cemetery. — The start of mourning; the Keriah; condolence visits: touching customs. — Departure; thoughts; a plan to return soon.

THE NEXT DAY, Wintzenheim regained its normal calm. Wedding guests from other places had left and the young bride had followed her new relatives to Bollwiller. As for the excellent, hospitable Papa Salomon, he had returned home with his family. I stayed behind in our village for a few days, as I still had many old acquaintances to see and was eager to explore the vicinity. This let me attend one final, sad rite of this Jewish life, having already witnessed many enthralling ceremonies in a very short period.

Returning from a hike in the countryside one evening, I learned that a long-expected disaster had struck the Marem family. The son of the poor *parness* had died. Rural Jews' grief is perhaps even more intense and direct than their joy, for Jews generally feel the loss of a relative more keenly than others do. We could find historical reasons for this. Persecuted for centuries and separated from the rest of society by insuperable barriers, they always had to seek comfort in the unity and joy of family as a shelter from external injustice. This explains the especially strong affection among family members and the acute affliction when they lose someone. Hadn't they drawn life from his life, rejoiced in his joys, suffered from his suffering? So, too, they died in a way with his death. Hence the touching funeral ceremonies among Jews.

As I entered the Marems' courtyard, I heard heart-rending cries. The mother and her two daughters were overcome with grief: I found them huddled behind the stove, their hair and clothes disheveled. They sometimes lurched into each other's arms and sometimes crouched on their chairs and rocked in a way unique to Eastern cultures during mourning. As soon as they saw me, they rushed over, wrapping their arms around my neck and redoubling their sobs. They had the same fits every time a friend or acquaintance entered. In an adjoining room, several rabbis sat around a circular table, chanting prayers. Poor Marem paced mechanically. He was not crying but his eyes and demeanor showed more pain than he could have expressed with a torrent of tears. Crowds of neighbors came and went. Through half-opened doors, you could occasionally see some poor people, attracted now by misfortune as they had been by the wedding festivities. Among country Jews, the poor are always looked after, both on sad days and happy ones.

Opposite us, I could see the room in which the child had died, where some good women were sewing the shroud. As custom requires, the deceased was laid out on a board at the foot of his bed. The day was spent in vain efforts to console the despairing family. When I briefly returned to my lonely room, I became lost in painful thoughts. What jolted me back to reality was two knocks on the shutters, repeated at intervals going off into the distance: the *shammes* was making his rounds to call people to the funeral. It was four in the afternoon. A throng heeding the funeral summons was on its way to the Marems', where we assembled in the courtyard. The last to arrive approached the others without greeting or talking to them, as there are no greetings or conversations in the home of the dead.

The Marem family was undergoing a terrible ordeal. I wish to describe the *Mechilah* ceremony[1] that occurs moments before the funeral procession. The *shammes* led all the relatives into the room where the boy had died. He lined them up facing the plank where the deceased lay, and invited the family to do its duty. One by one, these unfortunates leaned down over the plank and, after lifting the cloth that covered the body, took his icy feet in their hands. Stifled by tears, they stammered the prescribed formula, begging the departed to forgive them in eternity if they had ever mistreated him on this Earth. Then the coffin was nailed shut temporarily and the deceased, followed by all of us, was taken to the cemetery.

Unlike other funerals, Jewish ones involve no external show or pomp: no one sings hymns and there is nothing akin to a funeral mass. This simplicity might seem crude if it were not the expression of the sharpest, truest grief. The shoulders of four pallbearers carried a plain, unpol-

---

[1] Forgiveness ceremony.

ished coffin of light-colored wood draped in a black cloth. These men, whose head covering was no more ornate than a simple round hat, had been chosen by lot from a local religious society. Behind them came the dead boy's father, supported by two friends and staggering with anguish. The mother and both daughters accompanied the deceased only as far as the front door. Then they fainted and had to be taken back inside. The rest of the cortege—nearly all the Jews of Wintzenheim—followed pell-mell in no orderly manner, wearing everyday clothes.

They walked the length of the village, as the graveyard is at the far end. Passers-by stopped, silent and respectful.

The sky, grayish and dull, seemed to join in the general mourning. From atop the mountain looming over the hamlet and from the bottom of the valley, a melancholy fog—harbinger of the night—slowly spread its cloak over the village.

We heard only our own footsteps, punctuated sometimes by the *shammes* requesting alms for the poor in a solemn voice, and sometimes by the splash of water thrown onto the pavement. From each Jewish home along the route, people emptied the water from every container in the house into the street. This is because the water was doubly profaned. It was tainted by the passing of a corpse and by drops of blood that the Angel of Death might have left behind when wiping the blade of his liberating sword, as he hovered over the village since the previous day.

The small building at the entrance to the cemetery is called a *purification house*. The body was left there for final preparation. In sacred rites, it was washed with lukewarm water, the hair was combed and the nails cut, and it was covered in its shroud. A sort of scarf called a *tallith* was placed on its shoulders, its ends interlaced with the fingers to display on each hand the three Hebrew letters *shin, daled, yud,* spelling out the holy name of the Eternal One, God of the living and the dead.

On behalf of the *parness,* generous alms were given to the poor seated here and there on the graves, and the rabbi preached to the assembly. Once the coffin was closed and lowered into the ground, the *shammes* went to fetch unfortunate Marem. He would have the sad privilege of throwing the first shovels of soil over his child. We left the sacred enclosure. Before returning to the hamlet, the gathered group walked the length of the cemetery, pulling up handfuls of weeds that grew there all year and tossing them over their heads in bereavement.

Funeral rites and honoring the dead do not end there for rural Jews. The grief-stricken father was led home. Communal evening prayers took place in the house of the deceased, after which the mourning period began.

The furniture was moved aside and the mirrors covered in crepe. The mother and two girls removed their shoes and sat on the floor, their heads veiled. For the moment, they no longer wept or wailed. Their tears were exhausted, their voices nearly gone. The head of the family went to sit on a sack in a corner of the room, hiding his face in his hands. He could not savor his grief there for long; someone came to heighten it further. The *shammes* walked slowly towards him, tugged his arm gently and had him stand. He took a knife from his pocket, held a lapel of Marem's garment and cut it in two with a big, loud rip. This is known as the *Keriah* ceremony. The unhappy father let out a cry as if his heart had been torn at the same time, and dropped to the floor. Seeing this, the mother and daughters tried to rise from the floor where they were still seated. Defeated by this supreme effort, though, they fell back down prostrate. Touching and terrible scenes. Do we not recognize Biblical despair here? In the cries of these veiled women rolling on the ground, do we not hear something of the voice of "weeping and bitter lamentation" heard in Ramah when Rachel lost her children and refused to be comforted "because they are not here"?[2] This old man in torn garments seated on a sack is Job mourning his children; he is Jacob, a sackcloth upon his loins, his tunic in tatters, grieving for his favorite son.

As in ancient times, the period of deepest mourning lasts a full eight days. During these eight days, people send the family *mourning dishes* of broth and hard-boiled eggs. In these eight days, men and women of the congregation come to make condolence visits. You enter the mourning room without knocking, without saying hello. You seek a chair and sit near those you have come to console, matching your facial expressions to theirs, sighing to show you share their sorrow. You say nothing to them, however, unless they speak to you first. Then you talk with them only of the object of their grief. For eight

---

[2] Jeremiah 31:15.

Scene of mourning.

days, too, the community continues to pray together every morning and evening in the room where the death occurred. Near the deathbed, a long oil stain showing the size of the departed brings him constantly to mind. A night-light casts ominous reflections into the black recesses of the still-shuttered room and onto the afflicted relatives seated on the floor. Near this night-light sits a rustic terra-cotta cup filled with water. Throughout the mourning period, the deceased's soul comes to purify itself in this water twice a day before ascending to Heaven.

These are the scenes I beheld and impressions I gathered on this first brief journey to my native land. When I left that region of patriarchal mores and sturdy faith and had to return here to Paris (where for transplanted Alsatian Jews, our ancestors' religion and customs fade all too quickly into memory), I swore I would take the earliest opportunity for new pilgrimage to our Jewish Alsatian countryside. I wanted to reimmerse my soul in that simple life, the last vestige of a vanishing civilization of poignant customs, poetic traditions and gentle human warmth. These wedding festivities and funeral rites just days apart in one family felt like a vision of former times: a vision merry and sad by turns. It left me yearning for more visits to a society as worthy of sympathetic attention in times of joy as in times of woe. That wish came true sooner than expected. A few months later, I had the privilege to witness other distinctive scenes and ceremonies, which I shall share with the reader.

Rabbi teaching a Bible portion to a student.

PART II:

SPRING AND AUTUMN
JEWISH HOLIDAYS

CHAPTER ONE

Pesach or Passover; the matses. — Papa Salomon and his family again. — The Seder; Lazar the beggar; conversation. — The first and second day of Passover; Chol Hamoed; an excursion; a secret. — Departure. — The Omer.

RELIGIOUS HOLIDAYS are the main time when the ancient Hebrew civilization rises anew and, in a way, lives again in all its poetic grandeur. Just a year ago, I had the happy chance to return to Alsace during the four most solemn times of year for every good Jew. Friendly invitations brought me back to Haut-Rhin, first for the holidays of *Pesach* (Passover) and *Shavuoth* (Pentecost), and later for the observance of *Rosh Hashanah* (New Year) and *Yom Kippur* (the Day of Atonement), and lastly for the gracious celebration called *Sukkoth* (the Feast of Booths). I would therefore inhabit a Jewish world during the three most festive holidays of the year—Passover, Pentecost and the Feast of Booths—as well as the somber, fearsome days of *Rosh Hashanah* and *Yom Kippur*. I would spend time in a culture unknown to most readers, to which I was drawn by my oldest childhood memories. The scenes I encountered lived up to all my expectations.

My first stop would be in the village of Bollwiller, to visit the wonderful family that had welcomed me so warmly before: Papa Salomon's family. This fine, worthy old man was surrounded by a faithful mate and a young, flourishing brood: two pretty girls of the lovely Eastern type and three robust, alert lads. Under Papa Salomon's peaceful roof, I would spend Passover of 1858.

On the 14th day of the month of *Nisan* (March 29), I caught the Strasbourg-to-Basle train that would take me to Bollwiller, where I was expected around two in the afternoon. Gazing at the cheerful plains that the locomotive carried me past, I recalled a thousand customs, unchanged since the earliest eras of Jewish history, that give Passover its deep originality. This ancient, fascinating holiday was created to recall the Exodus from Egypt and the miraculous liberation of the Israelites, who, fleeing in great haste, took their bread dough with them before it even had time to rise! Hence the name *Feast of Unleavened Bread* and the tradition of eating *matses* during Passover. I still remembered the meticulousness of Alsatian Jews: surely exaggerating the intent of the Hebrew lawmaker,[1] they carefully remove all leaven from their homes two weeks before Passover. For half a month, there is such bustle and activity by the female population of each residence! From morning to night, it is all washing

---

[1] Expressed as follows in Exodus 12:15,18: "Seven days shall ye eat unleavened bread; but on the first day ye shall have put away leaven out of your houses. In the first month, on the fourteenth day of the month, at evening, ye shall eat unleavened bread, until the one and twentieth day of the month at evening. Seven days no leaven shall be found in your houses."

Making *matse* balls.

and cleaning. Pots and pans are heated red hot over a flame. Boiling water purifies gold and silver vessels for use during the holiday. When the week of cleaning begins, families' social relations are suspended so thoroughly that the Messiah himself, arriving in a Jewish village in Alsace, would run a great risk of finding every door closed. But the great day draws near at last! Starting on the day before the holiday, what a metamorphosis occurs indoors! Just marvel at those glorious garlands of onions and shallots spread over the plump bellies of ovens, and dozens of gleaming pewter plates arranged on the shelves for use only during Passover. Behold the dining room that doubles as a banquet hall. Festivity reigns and everything reflects flawless rustic elegance. The picture frames sparkle, especially the one around the *Mizrach* sign,[2] and white muslin curtains adorn all the windows. The freshly washed floor is covered in yellow and red sand. From every direction drifts the sweet scent of the first violets of the year. The inevitable seven-spouted lamp sways near the armchair-turned-throne (*lahne* in the local patois), strewn with spangled cushions on which the master of the house will recline on the first two nights of Passover. In these surroundings imbued with the ineffable charm of tradition, how could we not recall happy family scenes? How could we not think especially of the most characteristic pre-Passover ceremony: the baking of *matses* or unleavened bread, such a vital occupation among Jewish

---

[2] *Mizrach* means "East." The paper on which this word is written is placed in a frame. One turns to face *mizrach* when praying, since Jerusalem is to the east.

housewives in our countryside?[3] Once again I could imagine the huge table set up at six in the morning near the kitchen—that kitchen where a giant fire of sheaves has been burning in an open-front oven since the previous day. I remembered the laughter of hardy girls kneading the holy dough in shiny copper bowls, and the jeering of the workers who rolled it and pricked it and put it in the oven. These visions of the past cradled me as I arrived in the village where they would become today's realities.

As I crossed the street quickly, I noticed an early sign of the festival. Children walked through the village, each carrying a hamper filled with bottles. Their parents, wealthy *balbatim* (bourgeois), had told them to take fine wines to the rabbi, to the poor *Talmudists*,[4] to the *hazzan* (prayer leader), to the schoolteacher, to the *shammes* (the synagogue's beadle), etc. Shouldn't everyone be able to celebrate Passover with dignity and gaiety? Papa Salomon, meanwhile, had spotted me and came to meet me. We exchanged the classic greeting: "*Sholem aleichem* (Peace be with you)!" "*Aleichem sholem* (Peace be with you, too)!" I was soon surrounded by the whole family.

---

[3] In big cities, baking *matses* has become a business like any other. As Passover approaches, *matse* bakeries are set up under the direction of skilled individuals. The heads of these businesses hire men to go door to door several days before the festival, noting down how many pounds of unleavened bread each household will need for the eight days. Families do not have to bother baking their own *matses* since they will receive their supply in white baskets in time for the holiday.

[4] *Talmudists* are humble scholars who specialize in studying the Talmud and thus gain the right to practice various religious occupations. Some well-to-do families, for instance, pay them a salary to recite certain prayers, ensure their children's religious education, etc.

Workers baking *matses*.

My host's wife, kindly Yedele, and their daughters and sons received me with their usual cordiality. In a few words, they brought me up to date on the minor changes since my first stay at this quiet home in Bollwiller. Papa Salomon had retired. His eldest son had succeeded him and was now running the small business. It was Shemele who now made the purchases and sales, dealt with customers, and as far as I could tell, kept everyone happy. Pleasant and efficient, he was (his mother told me) loved and respected by everyone in Bollwiller and the neighboring villages. He was only twenty-three but several families had had their eye on him for some time, and more than one *shadshen* (matchmaker)[5] had already approached Papa Salomon.

But shall I be frank? The fate of those fine people was not foremost in my mind; I had come for a traditional Passover, celebrated according to the old rites. So my heart leapt when I heard the three knocks of the *shuleklopfer*,[6] which interrupted our conversation to call us to prayer. We all went to the splendidly illuminated synagogue, and after services each family returned home cheerfully. It was time for the *Seder*, the festival's defining ceremony, which deserves a faithful description.

My host's dining room was lit by the seven-spouted oil lamp. The table was set as if for supper, with plates and a white tablecloth but no utensils. On each plate was a booklet in Hebrew, illustrated with engravings showing

---

[5] Translator's note: *Shadchen* in modern Yiddish.
[6] *Synagogue knocker.* It is usually the *shammes* (beadle) who calls the faithful to services by knocking on doors with a wooden hammer.

A *Seder*.

the story of the Israelites' time in Egypt and the Exodus: this was the *Haggadah*, a collection of songs and prayers for the evening's ceremonies. Papa Salomon began by installing himself on his armchair–throne, and they placed me next to him in the seat of honor. On one side of the square table sat the mother and daughters, and across from them the sons. Like everyone else, the sons wore new clothes and had their heads covered according to custom, which is inflexible in this region. At the end of the table, I noticed a man with angular features in a rather battered hat and a frayed but spotless frock coat. He wore a yellow cotton neckerchief as a cravat. Salomon informed me that this was the family's usual guest for holy days: poor Lazare, a part-time beggar and part-time merchant who sold Hebrew prayer books at fairs for the Hebraic printers of Rodelheim and Soultzbach. Next to the poor man sat the big servant Hannah, a colorful figure with her hair thickly coated in rose pomade, wearing a plaid woolen shawl on her back for the occasion.

At the center of the table stood a silver dish holding three large pieces of unleavened bread separated by a napkin. Elevated above these three *matses* were little silver saucers containing an "exhibition" of the strangest-looking mix of disparate items: here some lettuce; there some fruit paste made with cinnamon, apples and almonds; further down, a goblet of vinegar; still further, sprigs of chervil, a hard-boiled egg and a bit of horseradish; and finally, next to these, a bone with a small amount of meat on it. These were a series of unsophisticated symbols, each with its own meaning and purpose. The fruit paste represented the clay, lime and brick that the Israelites used in their work when they were slaves to the Pharaohs. That vinegar, that hard-boiled egg, that horse-radish, that chervil stood for the bitterness and miseries of servitude. Lastly, that bone with a little meat on it symbolized the paschal lamb. A silver cup stood before each of us except the master of the house, whose cup was gold. On a shelf by the table sat a collection of carafes filled with the region's finest white wines, almost exclu-sively Kitterlé and Rangué. Oh, Kitterlé and Rangué, the Haut-Rhin's answer to Caecuban and Falernian wines! As tradition required, there were also several bottles of red wine. That evening, red wine was a reminder of the cruel-ty of the Pharaohs, who some people say bathed in the blood of Jewish children.

Meanwhile, Papa Salomon had begun the blessing that starts the holiday and the ceremony. The cups had been filled to the brim. After the prayer, the eldest son, Sheme-le, stood. He took a vase-shaped pitcher from a nearby table and poured water over his father's hands. On a sig-nal from our host, all the guests stood partway up and reached for the plate of unleavened bread. Then we pro-claimed these words that begin the *Haggadah*: "This is the bread of affliction which our ancestors ate in the Land of Egypt: let all that are hungry enter and eat; let all that are in want come hither and observe the Passover." The presence of Lazare the beggar at the table put that precept into practice in a touching way. The recitation continued. By custom, the household's youngest son then speaks, reading a question to the father in Hebrew from the

A simple *Seder* plate.

Haggadah: "What is the meaning of all this ceremony?" And the father replies, with his eyes fixed on the text of the *Haggadah* as well: "We were slaves unto Pharaoh in Egypt, and the Eternal, our God, brought us forth thence, with a mighty hand and an outstretched arm." We then each recited a detailed account of the Biblical story of the wondrous Exodus from Egypt, with all the miracles God performed for His people and all the blessings He bestowed on them. Next we sampled the symbolic objects displayed on the saucers and on the plate. Beside my host's cup on the table stood a much larger one that Salomon filled with his best wine. Whose cup was this? It was for Elijah the prophet: Elijah, that guiding spirit of Israel who is an unseen, ever-present guest at important ceremonies everywhere.

The first act of the *Seder* was over. The second act, the meal, began. As an observer, I merely noted the warm exuberance of this gathering and the dignified familiarity with which Lazare took part in conversations, put at ease by Papa Salomon's friendly questions. This beggar had been their guest on major holidays every year for a very long time! He had known these young adults as children. When answering or asking questions, Lazare called their father *Herr Salomon* (Mr. Salomon) but he called the daughters and sons by their given names alone. As I said, this small old man—a stunning personification of wandering Judea—combined his trade as a *shnorer* (beggar) with that of a Hebrew bookseller. In this dual capacity, he spent the whole year traveling from town to town, visiting all the boroughs and hamlets of Upper and Lower

Alsace. He also knew the Jewish world for some seventy miles around. Good Lazare was a roving journalist, a living chronicle. Salomon liked to have him speak at each holiday feast and Lazare did not mind repaying the hospitality in his own way and in his own currency, serving up all the news he had been able to gather during pauses in his rather vagabond existence.

"Well, Lazare!" said Papa Salomon suddenly, wishing to engage the beggar in conversation. "How is this *yontof* (holy day) treating you?"

"On my soul, Mr. Salomon, it's better to be here than on the open road. All year long I lead a hard life. But when *yontof* comes, I forget my troubles and drown them all in this good wine. It and I are old acquaintances."

And he drained his cup, which Shemele immediately refilled.

"And how's business?" continued Salomon.

"Don't ask! Would you believe it? These days, the books printed in Rodelheim and Soultzbach hardly sell. I used to sell piles of *Haggadahs* before Passover. Around *Rosh Hashanah* (New Year) and *Yom Kippur* (the Day of Atonement), when I worked the fairs, I had more requests than I could fill for collections of prayers for those important holidays. The factory trusted me. They sold them to me at a moderate fixed price, and I kept anything I could earn above that. But a while ago some people in Paris decided to publish French translations of the Bible, the daily prayer book, the *Haggadah*, and prayers for major festivals. I tell you, it's an abomination. Could God and would God want to hear prayers in any language but that of our ancestors in Palestine? The great *Bofel* (Babel) is where they print these gems. They send these abominable translations into all our villages, or 'gentlemen' like fat Getsch go out and hawk them. And to think, Mr. Salomon, most people who buy them don't understand French any better than you or me! But what can you do? It's fashionable, apparently. As sure as we have one God, creator of the world, and as sure as this is the first night of *Pesach* (Passover) for all Jews, all these changes can only bring misfortune. Who was it that lost *Yerusholayim* (Jerusalem)? The ungodly and the innovators, right? Wait and see: the ungodly and the innovators in Paris will keep us from returning there and rebuilding it, mark my words..."

The old beggar was about to launch into a kind of sermon, or rather a religious lament. Papa Salomon interrupted to ask for news of the countryside, and Lazare complied gladly. Most of the news was, of course, fairly trivial: the *hazzan* in Blotzheim had lost his voice after the recent holidays; the daughter of wealthy Lehmann Hirsch of Biesheim was going to marry a penniless former soldier in a story that was quite the "opera"—more about that later; the son of the *parness* (synagogue president) in Dornach had said something inappropriate to his fiancée and their wedding was canceled, and so on and so on. Lazare reported all this with jovial verve that made up for the sparse substance. I noticed, though, that when describing a boy in Rixheim whose sweetheart had broken off with him for some silly gaffe, Lazare made a pointed reference to Papa Salomon's eldest son.

"Of course you, Shemele," he said with a glint in his eye, "would never *pull such a goat* (make such a blunder). Words never fail you, and without meaning to flatter you, you've got what it takes to please the beauties in our villages. Also, by my soul, I've met some of them... You just leave it to Ephraim Schwab." Then, looking mischievously at all of us, he added, "A little bird tells me all sorts of things! What's more, little Deborah is a fine-looking girl... And old Nadel is very well off... Certainly of all the families in Hegenheim..."

"Enough chatter!" cut in the master of the house, half serious and half joking. "If we let you tell all your stories, we might forget to finish the *Seder*."

Everyone resumed their original attitude. The plate with the three *matses* wrapped in napkins was returned to the table, as were the symbolic objects. True to ancient custom, Papa Salomon took half a piece of unleavened bread from between the cushions of his chair, where he had placed it during the ceremony, and covered it with a napkin. This *matse* broken in two symbolized the crossing of the Red Sea. He gave a piece to each guest. We then recited the usual grace after meals, after which the third and final act of the *Seder* began.

"Shemele," said the father to his eldest son, "you may now open the door."

The young man rose from his seat, fully opened the door between the dining room and the hallway, and stood aside as if letting an important personage enter. There was utter silence. Moments later, the door was closed again. Someone had certainly entered, though invisibly. It was Elijah the prophet. He would now sip from the cup reserved for him and would bless the house with his presence. Elijah, multiplied infinitely, was at that moment entering every Jewish home where a *Seder* was being held. He was like God's representative. Our cups, emptied after the blessing, were refilled now for the fourth time. Next we sang some of the loveliest Psalms of David[7] to traditional melodies. We were still celebrating the miraculous Exodus and all the events before, during and after. In this pious concert, as we tried to outdo each other in zeal, spirit and voice, Lazare's impressive bass overpowered everyone else. Women, who must never sing in public among the Jews, lent their voices to the holy canticles at home that evening. Big Hannah, free from her duties, her thick red hands on her hips as she stood behind her mistress, was immersed in holy wonderment. The singing continued and the libations became more and more copious. This is customary. At nine o'clock, the women withdrew and the men stayed at their posts. That evening, Jews do not recite the usual prayer before bed. It is understood that this night and the next are special nights on which God watches over all Jewish homes, as in ancient Egypt. Little by little under the growing influence of the Rangué and Kitterlé wines, amid the final traditional recitations, the men's eyes began to glaze. Voices trailed off and heads lolled. It was bedtime, time to go our separate ways. Entering my room, I told myself that Papa Salomon's home certainly did need divine protec-

---

[7] Psalms 115, 116, 118 and 156. [Translator's note: There is no Psalm 156. He may mean Psalm 136, the Great Hallel.]

tion that night since that fine man and his guests seemed in no condition to keep watch.

The *Seder* ceremony is repeated identically the next evening at the same hour: at nightfall. That date and the next, the 15th and 16th of the month of *Nisan* (March 30 and 31), are a major festival. Jews go to synagogue early in the morning, and men and women are pleased to show off their freshly made outfits. It is a pleasure to see these good people travel the streets of the village, pressed and starched. They eat a big meal at midday and spend the afternoon making or receiving visits. Salomon's prominence in the community meant he was one of those who awaited visitors. In this context in Alsace, one receives family and friends at the table, where the head of the house and his family sit until evening prayers. Dessert remains on the table and is replaced throughout the afternoon as guests consume it. All new arrivals are met promptly with this hospitable greeting: *Boruch habo* (blessed be the person arriving)! They are invited to sit at the table, and the maidservant immediately pours them a glass of the region's best wine. Around two thirty, the room we were in was nearly full. The noise of the conversations was deafening. There was my host's brother Yekel along with numerous relatives, the neighbor Samuel, the *hazzan*, the teacher from the community school, and the *shammes* of Bollwiller. What topics made up that boisterous mishmash of conversation? It would be hard to say. In fact, the people around me discussed a bit of everything. It was simultaneously about politics, railroads, synagogues newly built or soon to be built, consistorial board elections, nominations of *parnosim* (synagogue presidents), and the cattle markets in Lure and in Saint-Dié. Eventually, the cuckoo clock in the corner crowed four o'clock and the gathering broke up to go to *Mincha* (afternoon prayer).

Passover, like the Feast of Booths, lasts eight days, but only four of those eight are major holy days. The four in between are semi-holy days known as *Chol Hamoed* and are of a particular nature. During *Chol Hamoed*, men forego big business transactions and perform only day-to-day operations. The women, somewhat dressed up, do not work but pay visits or go walking outside the village or in neighboring villages. The days of *Chol Hamoed* are also when beaus visit their sweethearts and when Jewish betrothals generally take place.

On the first of these semi-holy days, Papa Salomon had taken me in a *char-à-bancs* pulled by his little gray horse to the nearby town of Dornach to visit a relative of his. Towards evening, we returned to Bollwiller. Papa Salomon happily smoked *violet* tobacco from his *yontof* pipe and had the little horse trot us back to the village. My host was eager to confide in me about the future he dreamed of for his son Shemele.

"Where are you planning to spend next *Shavuoth* (Pentecost)?" he asked abruptly.

"Why, right in Biesheim, at Lehmann Hirsch's house."

"Perfect," he replied. "Hirsch is expecting his future son-in-law during that holiday. For as you know, in Alsace, young men typically visit their fiancées at that time of year. Besides, Hirsch is your friend and he'll tell you the story behind that marriage. People have talked about it enough, *boruch Hashem* (thank God)! After all that talk, they'll simply have to get married."

Clearly, Papa Salomon had not yet found the transition he was seeking.

He added, "And where will you be during *Sukkoth* (the Feast of Booths)?"

On this topic, chance would serve him better.

I told him I planned to accept an invitation to spend the holiday at the home of little Aron, a watch merchant in Hegenheim.

"Ah!" he cried. "You'll spend *Sukkoth* at my friend Aron's... in Hegenheim?" Then he continued with a mysterious smile, emphasizing every word: "Well, then! It's not inconceivable that we will be in Hegenheim as well... during the *Chol Hamoed* of *Sukkoth*..."

"Say, Papa Salomon," I replied, struck by a sudden thought. "Was Lazare the beggar correct the other night at the *Seder*? Might his little bird have given him an accurate tip?"

"Do I have any secrets from you?" Papa Salomon replied solemnly. The old man slowed the horse to a walk, reached into the big pocket of his coat, took out an immense wallet, opened it and removed a large letter that he unfolded slowly while continuing to puff tobacco smoke loudly from his pipe. Handing me the letter, he said, "Read it."

This important message, written in magnificent *Yiddish* characters, was addressed to Papa Salomon from the *shadshen* (matchmaker) Ephraim Schwab.[8] It gave a glowing report on the Nadel family of Hegenheim, with whom my host planned to form a marital alliance. What better match could there be for young Shemele than the only daughter of wealthy Nadel, beautiful Deborah, "with large eyes like a sparrow hawk's and a complexion of roses and lilies," to speak like Ephraim Schwab! "Your Shemele," concluded the *shadshen*, "can make a trip to Hegenheim during the *Chol Hamoed* of *Sukkoth*. He will stay with your friend little Aron to avoid gossip. I shall go to Hegenheim around that time. You choose the day. I shall accompany Shemele to the Nadel home. If you wish, I shall write to them and the matter will be settled. As for the *shadshonnes* (matchmaker's fees), we shall reach an agreement. I have arranged many a marriage in my life and I have never had a falling out with anyone, thank goodness! People know Ephraim Schwab."

"And what have you decided?" I asked Papa Salomon as I handed back the letter.

"I find it a suitable match. I only trusted information from my friend Aron, who said to proceed with confidence. So my Shemele will go you-know-where on the first day of the *Chol Hamoed* of *Sukkoth*. You'll be there then, too, and if all goes well, you'll be a guest on the bridegroom's side."

We returned to the house by seven o'clock. Three days later, Passover week was over and Papa Salomon and his

---

[8] Jewish marriages rarely occur without the intervention of this specialized agent, who charges fees for each successful negotiation. At one time, it was quite a lucrative profession.

wife and Shemele took me to the Bollwiller train station. While awaiting *Shavuoth* (Pentecost), I traveled back to spend time in the great Babel, as Lazare the beggar called it. As Papa Salomon shook my hand, he urged me to travel cautiously since it was now the *Omer*. This word reminded me of one of our Jewish folk superstitions. My journey to Alsace had been filled with old memories of Passover, but now the trip home brought back countless recollections of the *Omer*.

"So, what is the *Omer*?" you are probably asking. It is the time between Passover and Pentecost. The Jewish Pentecost marks the anniversary of receiving the Ten Commandments, a revelation that happened, as you know, *seven weeks* after the Israelites left Egypt. That is why Pentecost is also called *Shavuoth*, a Hebrew word meaning "weeks." In bygone days in Jerusalem, people initiated the period from the second day of Passover to Pentecost by going to the Temple and making an offering of one measure (*omer*) of barley. Today there are no more offerings. Instead, from *Pesach* to *Shavuoth*, all the faithful in the village count the days of that period every evening after prayers, once night has fallen.[9] They thus show their eagerness to reach the festival of the giving of the Law. Country Jews consider the *Omer* a dreadful period in which a thousand extraordinary things happen.

To understand the kind of mysterious terror that hovers over this period will require some explaining.

The famous Rabbi Akiva flourished in Jerusalem in the

---

[9] Hence the *Omer* is also called *Sefirah* (counting).

time of Emperor Hadrian. Akiva had many disciples. Now, it happened one year between *Pesach* and *Shavuoth* that most of the pious rabbi's disciples died suddenly. This plunged all of Israel into a grief that apparently still echoes today. Some purely local Alsatian beliefs and prejudices have become attached to this tradition over time: During the *Omer*, every Jewish child is especially vulnerable to the powers and whims of evil spirits. During the *Omer*, such spirits' influence is felt everywhere; something dangerous and fateful is in the air. You must be vigilant and not tempt the *sheydim* (demons) in any way or they will play nasty tricks on you. During the *Omer*, you must be careful of everything, even the most seemingly banal, insignificant things. Listen to a few of the detailed recommendations made even today, at the height of the nineteenth century, by Jewish housewives at this time of year: Children, don't whistle after dark during the *Omer* or your mouth will become deformed; don't go out in shirtsleeves or your arms will be maimed; don't throw stones in the air or they'll fall on you; avoid firing guns because the shot will wound you instead. Men of all ages should not travel by horse, carriage or boat during the *Omer*: the horse will try to throw you, the carriage's wheels could break, even if it is new, and the boat will surely capsize. Above all, watch over your animals, as this is the main time when *machsheves* (witches) sneak into your barns, climb onto the backs of cows and goats, strike them ill, lay them on the ground and corrupt their milk. Incidentally, if that happens, you'll need to try to capture the suspect and lock her in a room where you have taken the precaution to place some of the milk she corrupted into a bucket. Next, whip the milk with a hazel switch while uttering the Lord's name three times. While whipping the milk, you will hear cries and wailing. That will be the witch moaning, for every blow of the switch on the milk will actually strike her. Now keep whipping until blue flames dance on the milk. Only then will the spell be broken, but it is better not to give witches time to cast their hexes in the first place. So if a beggar woman appears at nightfall during the *Omer* to ask a family for a few embers to light her poor hearth, they should not give her what she wants. But before letting her leave, they should always tug at one of her skirts three times and then right away, without a moment's pause, throw big handfuls of salt into the flame in the fireplace. The beggar might be a witch, for *machsheves* make any excuse to enter homes and they use every kind of disguise.

Such are the hazards of the *Omer*. Now you will comprehend the sage recommendations of my host in Bollwiller. Need I mention that I followed them to the letter? I arrived in Paris without the engine exploding and without the car jumping the track. And since I made sure not to stick my nose or arm out the door, I arrived unwounded and unbruised. That is the advantage of not tempting the *sheydim*.

Making *frimsel* (egg noodles).

CHAPTER TWO

Lehmann Hirsch; an "opera." — The village of Biesheim; Rachel and Meyerle. — The festival of Shavuoth (Pentecost). — A devout, touching ceremony; explanation. — Gifts. — Dancing. — Departure. — Present and future.

ALMOST SEVEN WEEKS had passed. I was therefore about to go to Biesheim, a small village on the banks of the Rhine, three leagues from Colmar. This is where Lehmann Hirsch the horse dealer lives. Biesheim (where the reader will soon join me) is, in fact, where I would celebrate...

> The hallowed day
> On which upon Mount Sinai unto us
> The Law was given.[1]

Lehmann Hirsch, another old friend of my family, lived in such great rustic comfort that the locals considered him rich. Hirsch arrived in Colmar ahead of me so he could take me to Biesheim in his *char-à-bancs*. He

---

[1] Translator's note: From the first scene of Racine's *Athalie*, quoted here from J. Donkersley's English translation.

wore his traditional costume: leather-trimmed trousers, oiled boots adorned with spurs, and a long gray frock coat around which a superb whip was wrapped like a bandoleer. This item, a crucial symbol of his profession, would have been the envy of any rider at the Cirque Olympique in Paris.

We set out for Biesheim in the afternoon. Lehmann's *char-à-bancs* was overpacked with baskets and crates containing a whole menagerie of poultry and a whole garden of vegetables and early fruits, all freshly bought in Colmar.

"Hirsch," I said as I sat down next to him, "I would give you a good telling off if I seriously thought you'd gone to such excess just to welcome me for this short holiday of *Shavuoth*! Please tell me it's not for me but for your future son-in-law that you've spent all this money. I know you're expecting him for both days of *Shavuoth*."

"Let's not discuss that!" said Hirsch, answering the first half of my comment. Then he added, "Yes, it's true, I'm expecting my daughter's fiancé for *Shavuoth*. He'll arrive on the eve of the holiday: the day after tomorrow in the afternoon. But who in the world told you? I was hoping to surprise you!... Wait, I know... Papa Salomon said something. Did he at least tell you all of it?"

"No," I replied. "He only said there was quite a story behind this marriage."

"He wasn't lying. I swear, it's been like the plot of an opera. I laugh and joke now that the deal is done, but there was a moment, believe me, when I wasn't laughing! At first I was afraid of losing my daughter, and after that,

I wouldn't listen to reason. But when women get an idea into their head, it's darned difficult to... Oh, well, what can you do?! I gave in and I don't regret it. When you love your children as much as we do, don't you let them have their way? Again, I don't regret it. It was written and ordained that my Rachel should be happy in the future, and I believe she will be. The rest hardly matters."

"Even so, Papa Hirsch, I don't know the story. Go on, it's an hour and a half from here to Biesheim. You can bring me up to date. I'll listen with interest and pleasure."

"Goodness, it won't take long to tell," Hirsch said after lighting his pipe. "Here's what happened. The late Brendel Ulmann, my mother-in-law, lived in Marmoutier. One day when she was already quite old, she asked us to send our little Rachel to be raised in her home. She loved the girl dearly and besides, Rachel could keep her company. Rachel was ten at the time. It was a hard choice for my wife and me because, let me tell you, she was a sweet little girl. But finally, to make her *fralleh* (grandmother) happy, we agreed. Rachel went to school in Marmoutier and was always top of her class in *Chumesh* (Pentateuch), which she still knows by heart. After school she would stay with her *fralleh*, who taught her housekeeping. After a while, my mother-in-law no longer did any housework at all. Rachel was young but she kept the little household running. My mother-in-law saw no one in the village except her neighbor Jonas, a bric-a-brac dealer. He was very attached to her, for my mother-in-law was good and kind to Jonas. She often lent him a bit of money to sustain his poor little business, which his wife's illness and death had nearly ruined. Jonas always brought along Meyerle, his little boy, who was just five years older than my Rachel. I, of course, knew nothing of this until much later, but it seems the two children took to each other quickly. Meyerle, who knew how good my mother-in-law had been to his father, made a point to be as helpful as possible to his neighbors: In the morning and evening, he would come to take my mother-in-law to synagogue and home again. When Rachel was a school-girl, every day at three, he would bring her a mid-afternoon snack in a little basket, and in winter, when there was ice on the ground, he would wait for her. Once Rachel grew up, Meyerle came to help her with the housework whenever his father's trade allowed. He would install himself in the kitchen, wash her dishes for her, peel her onions, clean her herbs, and in the evening, he would go with her to the fountain to draw water. Then, each holding one handle, they would carry the bucket of water back to the house. Especially on Fridays (when, as you know of old, there are twice as many chores in our homes), Meyerle never failed to lend my daughter a hand. That day, he would run every errand and do every task for her: once the ingredients were combined for the next day's meals, he would take the pans to the baker's and put them in the oven;[2] he would buy fish,[3] pick up spices, prepare the lamp wicks, and, in appreciation, Rachel, on her *fralleh*'s behalf, often invited him and his father for

---

[2] As you know, the Law of Moses prohibits handling fire on Friday evening or Saturday.

[3] An essential dish on Friday evenings among Alsatian Jews.

Friday evening dinner. My mother-in-law saw no problem with that, and ultimately, there was none. However, as they grew up, the two children became more and more fond of each other and began to feel a wisp of love, so to speak. My mother-in-law smiled on all this and never alerted me. Old people are like that. By then, Rachel had turned sixteen and Meyerle was about to turn twenty-one.

"The military draft began and Meyerle lost. He drew number 17. Jonas was poor, as I said, and could not pay for another man to take his place. Meyerle prepared to leave and join the Zouaves.[4] The day of his departure, his poor father and my mother-in-law wept. My Rachel dreaded the separation more than anyone but she never cried, at least not in front of Meyerle. As she later told me, she did not want to dishearten him. Accompanied by Papa Jonas, she took our conscript to Strasbourg where, in front of Jonas, she gave him a bag containing *tefillin* (phylacteries) as well as a prayer book bound in green morocco leather. She advised Meyerle to never forget the good Lord while serving in the Army, to always pray sincerely, to stay a good Jew, and if the occasion arose, to show the courage she knew he had, as befits a Frenchman. Rachel said that on his return, Meyerle should bring back the *tefillin* bag and prayer book, but in the meantime he should keep them as a reminder. When a tearful Meyerle responded that *seven years* of service and ab-

---

[4] Translator's note: Zouaves were companies of French light infantry, originally recruited from African countries that France had invaded and colonized. By the time of this story, Zouave units also included European French soldiers.

sence was quite long, guess how this young woman replied. Ah, you see she knew her *Chumesh* (Bible) just as
well as she knew her parents! She replied that the patri-
arch Jacob, too, had done seven years' service for another
Rachel. Meyerle, she said, should emulate him, for she
promised to wait for his discharge from the Army and not
become engaged to anyone but him.

"Meyerle left. A few months later, after my poor moth-
er-in law died, Rachel moved back to Biesheim.

"Years passed and my wife and I suspected nothing.
Rachel always wrote to Meyerle in secret and he addressed his replies to our *Shabbes goye*,[5] old Catherine.
Meanwhile, I dreamed of finding a husband for my
daughter. *Shadshonim* (matchmakers), I can tell you,
came and went, and many times Ephraim Schwab, whom
you surely know by name, suggested wonderful matches
for her. But Rachel always refused, claiming she did
not want to marry. By then, after five years, Meyerle had
left Africa to join the troops in the Crimea, and once he
debarked, old Catherine received no more of his letters
to the girl. That is also when my poor Rachel began
visibly fading away. She fell gravely ill with a malignant
fever and I thought she would die. One day when I
returned from the horse show in Haguenau, Rachel was
in bed. I went to her and began to cry when I saw her
misery and suffering. Then she took my hand and said
that while I was away, she had told her mother everything. And in turn, Rachel told me the story you now

[5] A non-Jewish woman who, in every household, handles work that the
Law of Moses forbids Jews from doing on the Sabbath.

know. She added that she loved Meyerle and that the lack of news since he left for the Crimea, together with all her distress during his absence, had made her ill. She said she knew Jonas was poor and Meyerle had nothing, but she preferred Meyerle with nothing to anyone else with property and money; that if Meyerle was dead, she would not survive him; and that if I loved her, I must not try to stand in her way. Then she begged me to have someone write to the Crimea and find out from Meyerle's comrades what had become of him. Naturally enough, I found this doubly upsetting, but I swear that what mattered most to my wife and me was our child, and we promised her we would do everything she asked. From that day, my poor Rachel recovered slowly until a very pleasant surprise restored her strength and health. Two weeks later, Papa Jonas, who knew of my daughter's love for his Meyerle, showed up at our house one morning, out of breath.

"'You don't know,' he shouted as soon as he saw my daughter. Rachel had told him of the promise we'd made to her. 'You don't know? We've had a letter from Meyerle. He's very well. He was lucky. He got through the siege of Malakoff without a mark on him... No, I'm wrong. The mark he ended up with was... the red ribbon. Yes, on my soul! He was awarded the red ribbon!'

"Meyerle had saved two wounded comrades whom three Russian soldiers had wanted to finish off, according to his letter to his father. At this news, my poor Rachel fainted with joy.

"When she came to, she said, 'I just knew Meyerle would distinguish himself and that my *tefillin* and little prayer book would bring him luck and bring him home to us safe and sound.'

"Six months later, Meyerle returned from the Crimea with his final discharge. Eight days after that, he was engaged to my Rachel. They'll be married after the High Holidays, at the start of winter. My daughter is twenty-three and her fiancé twenty-eight. The day after tomorrow, Meyerle will come to spend the two days of *Shavuoth* with us and with his fiancée, as is customary. You'll see him then, my dear friend, and that pleases me, because although he has nothing he's still a fine boy. You wanted all the details and now you know everything. Wasn't I right when I said this is a regular 'opera'?"

I had to agree and I think the reader would have agreed, too, in my place.

We arrived moments later in Biesheim. My friend Lehmann Hirsch's wife and daughter awaited us at the threshold of the house. Rachel was a picture of shapely rural Jewish beauty. Her features and big, lovely dark eyes expressed sweetness and resolve at the same time. She greeted me in the Alsatian manner, laughing. The laughter was all the more charming because it revealed two rows of exquisitely white teeth.

"Meyerle," I thought, "is a very lucky man."

My host's home showed signs of preparation for the approaching festival and the fiancé. Everything was clean, tidy, gleaming.

The next day around noon, the pavement of the only road in Biesheim resounded with the noise of a *char-à-bancs* carriage weighed down by an acacia trunk. Driving this vehicle himself was a young man with a handsome face, a bronzed complexion and a formidable mustache. He wore a long waistcoat and flat cap, but under that very bourgeois attire you would recognize him as a military man. This was our Meyerle, former Zouave, late of Africa and the Crimea, the happy fiancé of faithful Rachel. The afternoon sped past with conversations of all kinds and preparations of every type. *Shavuoth* would begin that evening. The *kalleh* (bride) and her mother spent half an hour going through all the rooms and staircases in the house, literally strewing them with the traditional greenery, roses, tulips and marjoram in honor of *Shavuoth*.

That evening after synagogue and before supper, the *chosn* (bridegroom) gave his *kalleh* several customary gifts: Rachel received a pair of earrings, a red scarf and a parasol.

Hirsch, in turn, as future father-in-law, gave Meyerle the traditional silver watch and gold snuffbox. In our countryside, regardless of whether the groom "partakes" or not, the snuffbox is essential. The meal that followed was, of course, as impeccable in every way as the meals we would enjoy over the next days.

Visitors filed in that evening and stayed. They had come to say *sholem aleichem* to the bridegroom.

Despite his modesty and though they already knew about it, Meyerle had to tell everyone of his heroics in the

Crimea and show his glorious red ribbon to everybody who was touching and prodding him.

Early the next morning before synagogue, we witnessed a special religious scene that I should mention here, which lasted until we were inside the sanctuary. Because *Shavuoth* marks the anniversary of receiving the Ten Commandments, this is the day wealthy villagers always choose for donating a new *Torah* to the synagogue in honor of some wish that has been granted. The *Sefer* (scroll of the Holy Book), handwritten in beautiful Hebrew letters by some steadfast rabbi, was displayed on a makeshift Mt. Sinai in the donor's home and then taken to the synagogue on *Shavuoth* morning with great pomp. One of Hirsch's neighbors, big Hertz, was endowing the synagogue with a *Torah* that day, honoring the recovery of a son who had nearly died. The village was aflutter. The procession left Hertz's house at eight o'clock. Under a holy canopy, the rabbi carried the *Sefer*, flanked by the donor and the *hazzan* (prayer leader). The whole community, men and women in full dress, walked behind them to the rhythm of earnestly joyous music that played at the front of the procession. Hirsch and his future son-in-law—the latter in a green frock coat and chocolate-brown trousers—had joined the crowd.

We slowly reached the

> Temple, festooned everywhere
> With magnificent adornments.[6]

---

[6] Translator's note: From the first scene of Racine's *Athalie*.

The tabernacle and holy platform were surrounded by moss and flowers. After the habitual prayer, the *hazzan* placed the new *Sefer* on the platform, unrolled it and read the usual chapters as if to inaugurate it. As the bridegroom, Meyerle had the great honor of being "called" to the *Torah*[7] before the reading of one such chapter. The open *Sefer* was then rolled up and covered with a precious silk mantle, also supplied by the generous donor. Then it was placed in the Holy Ark that holds the ancient scrolls of the Law. The *hazzan* kissed these scrolls respectfully, asking them on our behalf to accept the new holy occupant in their midst without envy—a candid, moving, noteworthy gesture.

After the official prayers, the book of Ruth was recited. Why? I think this is the reason: In Jerusalem, *Shavuoth* was not just a religious holiday but also an agricultural one, marking the gathering of wheat. The story of Ruth the gleaner is probably meant to evoke that, for it is about fields and the harvest. Yes, the book of Ruth: that delightful, charming eclogue, fresh and happy as nature itself at the season of poetic Pentecost!

The ceremony was, of course, complemented that evening by a great gala at big Hertz's house. After spiritual pleasures, physical pleasures!

If anything, that first afternoon of *Shavuoth* brought an even steadier stream of visitors to the Hirsch home than the previous evening. Meyerle sat next to his dear and beautiful *kalleh*, Rachel, who beamed with happiness. The couple's gifts to each other were paraded before

---

[7] "Called": In German, *aufgerufen*.

the guests, who each congratulated them differently. One said to Meyerle, "No matter what, you were lucky to find a pearl like Rachel. To think she waited seven whole years for you! Are there many with such patience?" Another added, "How lovely to marry a *chosn* who wears the red ribbon! Do you know, Rachel, that when you go to Colmar with your *chosn*, soldiers will present arms to him in front of the prefecture, at the General's Gate, at the courthouse, anywhere with a sentry on duty? Won't you feel proud then? It really is wonderful!"

These words echoed delightfully in the ears of our friend Hirsch and his worthy wife. Meyerle, whom they had long rejected, was now a source of pride. His gift to her, for he had no assets to offer, was the esteem that surrounded him.

The next day after dinner, there was a dance in the couple's honor. The young people of Biesheim had arranged this tribute and had brought in musicians from Gueberschwihr. The orchestra stopped at the Hirsch home to pick up the bride and bridegroom and begin the procession. By popular demand and at Rachel's express wish, Meyerle went through the village in his Zouave uniform, which he had made a point to pack in his black trunk. You should have seen him in his turban, his baggy trousers, his long gaiters, and his waistcoat on which a Legion of Honor cross now glittered in the May sun! Every window was open along the dancers' route. With satisfaction, Hirsch and his wife stood on their doorstep with their arms folded, watching the merry troupe move away.

The next day, I took leave of these good people. I had to promise Rachel and the hero of the Crimea that I would attend their wedding. Circumstances, however, would prevent me from keeping that promise. So let me tell you quickly what became of our hero and heroine. Meyerle and Rachel are married now. Hirsch gave up his horse-dealing business, which Meyerle did not want.

Meyerle preferred farming. It was more suited to his way of seeing things. He is successfully farming a few acres near Biesheim—the classic French soldier-laborer.

Alsatian Jews in cotton caps at synagogue
between *Rosh Hashanah* services.

CHAPTER THREE

Selichot week: defining traits; a ghost. — Rosh Hashanah (New Year); various ceremonies; the shofar and the shofar blower; prayer written by a dying martyr. — Yom Kippur; the kapporah; another curious custom; Yom Kippur Eve; an incident; holy day for the dead; two old prayers. — The Aaronites' blessing. — Nehillah.

WE HAVE ALREADY SEEN the special nature of Passover: It is both a family celebration and a holy day. One of its main ceremonies, the *Seder*, occurs in the home, and preparing for Passover involves a thousand domestic chores. *Shavuoth* (Pentecost) is much the same: It has an equally strong domestic element, as families celebrate it at home and invite friends and relatives to join them. *Shavuoth* is also when betrothed couples generally visit.

Totally different from these are the holy days in September and October that begin the Jewish year: *Rosh Hashanah* (New Year) and *Yom Kippur* (Day of Atonement). Do you wish to see Jews at synagogue? Would you witness the austere grandeur of the rites that inaugurate each year in a season of unchanging traditions? Once again, the place to be is in one of these curious Jewish villages in Alsace. Follow us, for instance, into the honest, pious population of Wintzenheim. That is where we beheld all the scenes typical of this season of penitence, and where we spent the mysterious week of *Selichoth*[1] that precedes *Rosh Hashanah*. True believers hold that *Selichoth* coincides with an especially potent intrusion of supernatural forces into human affairs.

Anyone approaching Wintzenheim at three in the morning during *Selichoth* would find the people up and walking to synagogue, heeding the call of the *shammes* (beadle) who has crossed the village, wordlessly knocking three times on various surfaces with his wooden hammer—tapping now on a shutter, now on a carriage gate. The prayers last until dawn. Who can tell what fearsome encounters the *shammes* and *hazzan* (prayer leader) must expose themselves to on their nightly rounds as they walk to the house of God? *Selichoth* is the season of hauntings and apparitions. How often does the *shammes* hear sepulchral voices mix with the sound of wind stirring the weeping willows in the cemetery! How often does the *hazzan* see tongues of fire lighting the darkness before him, or dreadful phantoms blocking his way! At social gatherings after dark, everyone in Wintzenheim talks of the spirit that appeared one night during *Selichoth* some thirty years ago to terrify Chief Rabbi Hirsch, of blessed and venerable memory. The rabbi lived very near the synagogue. The ritual bath for women's ablutions was located in his house and, as it were, under his

---

[1] A Hebrew word meaning "forgiveness," because of the prayers one says every morning to invoke God's forgiveness.

safekeeping. It was night. The rabbi, with his *Gemara*[2] open in front of him, was engrossed in that sacred book. Outside, all was calm and quiet. Suddenly he hears a pitiful voice from the courtyard under the window. The rabbi opens the window and sees a white ghost holding out its hands, pleading. "What do you want?" asked the rabbi. "I," the ghost replied, "am the wife of Faisel Gaismar. They buried me yesterday. I was ill for six weeks and unable to go to the *mikve* (ritual bath) last month, and am therefore forced to return. Rabbi, be so good as to give me the keys to the *mikve*." Without hesitating, the rabbi tosses the heavy bunch of keys to the supplicant. Moments later, he hears the water lapping and can make out the exact moment when she plunges in and gets out, wringing her soaked hair each time. Silence returns. The rabbi continues studying his *Gemara* and around two o'clock, he dozes off on the sacred volume. At three, he was awoken by the *shammes*'s wooden hammer calling him to *Selichoth* prayer. As he left, he spied the *mikve* keys hung in their usual spot by the door.

But the last night of *Selichot* is done. Next comes a whole series of deeply austere holy days. Let me describe them without leaving the synagogue, rather than relating mundane incidents from my stay with one of Wintzenheim's most strictly observant families. It is *Rosh Hashanah* morning and here we are in a modest village synagogue. The large congregation is rapt in prayer and will worship from dawn until around ten in the morning.

---

[2] Commentary on the *Mishna* (code of traditional laws), which together with this code makes up the Talmud proper.

Then in profound silence, the *hazzan* opens the doors of the Holy Ark and draws out the *Torah* (sacred scroll of the Law). Having chanted the customary words of glorification, he carries the sacred scroll onto the rostrum in the middle of the synagogue and unrolls the *Torah*. The people listen as the *hazzan*, to an ancient melancholy melody, begins to recite the Hebrew that describes the calling of Abraham and the binding of Isaac at this time of year. The Jews remind God that this sacrifice cemented an eternal covenant with Him, and this enduring memory is what encourages them to beg Him for mercy and help.

When the reading ends, the sounding of the *shofar* begins.

So, what is a *shofar*?

It is a curved horn measuring a foot and a half in length, made specifically from a ram's horn in memory of the ram sacrificed in place of Isaac. The Israelites used the *shofar* in all their religious and military ceremonies. The blast of the *shofar* brought down the walls of Jericho; the blast of the *shofar* announced the new moon and major festivals in olden times; it is also the blast of the *shofar* that God, at the end of time, will use to call the faithful from the bottom of their graves and bring them back to Jerusalem. And so on this day of remembrance, the *shofar* ceremony is meant to inspire a wholesome terror in the soul.

Not just anyone may blow the *shofar* in our synagogues. It must be a pious man of pure morals. In Wintzenheim, the Talmudist *Reb*[3] Koschel has fulfilled that duty for forty years. When the moment arrives, Reb

---

[3] Corruption of the word "rabbi."

Koschel walks gravely across the rostrum where the rabbi awaits. Each of them now wraps his head in his silken prayer shawl called a *tallith*. After a short prayer, Reb Koschel takes the *shofar* from its white cloth pouch. "Blessed art Thou, O Lord our God!" he says. "Blessed art Thou, King of the Universe, who hath sanctified us with Thy commandments and ordered us to sound the *shofar!*" These words herald the sounding of the sacred horn, and all eyes lower immediately for no one must see the person blowing the *shofar*. Reb Koschel brings the ram's horn to his mouth and awaits the rabbi's orders: "*Tekiah* (trumpet blast)!" cries the rabbi, and a metallic sound answers his command. "*Shevorim* (breakings)," and the *shofar* emits a sort of faltering moan. "*Teruah* (clarion call)," and the sound trembles and accelerates.

Each command is executed several times until the *shofar* has issued *twenty-nine* sounds. After the final one, the sacred scroll is returned to the Holy Ark amid singing. A new service begins. The *hazzan*, alone or joined by the voices of the congregation, recalls the origin and purpose of "this holy day of convocation." Today the whole universe stands before God. Today it will be decided "who shall be happy, who shall not, who shall have war, who shall have peace." God will be good and merciful to His people for the sake of the patriarchs and for His own sake, in remembrance of all He did for His people, from the Egyptian Exodus to their arrival in the land of Canaan! At one point, people prostrate themselves on the floor to beg the Almighty for mercy. Next come the triple *Sanctus* and traditional *Hosanna* known as the *Kedushah* (sanctification), preceded by a marvelous, famous passage written, they say, by the martyr Rabbi Amnon of Mayence.[4]

First, a word about Rabbi Amnon.

Rabbi Amnon lived in the sixteenth century in Mayence.[5] He is the hero of one of the most moving legends of Jewish martyrology, so rich in woeful tales. The learned Amnon was received at the court of the prince-elector of Mayence, who held him in great esteem. The chroniclers say that this sealed his doom, for one day the prince offered to make the rabbi his chief advisor if only he would renounce his religion. After resisting insistent entreaties for months, Amnon finally asked for three days to think it over. He immediately berated himself for his weakness. After three days and more refusals, he was taken by force to the prince. "When I asked you for three days," Amnon said, "it was like denying my God. Let the tongue that uttered those rash words be torn out. That is the punishment I would give myself." The prince rejected this ruling. The tongue, he said, had spoken well, but the feet that refused to come to him should be cut off. To refine the cruelty, the prince also wanted Amnon to lose his arms. This horrifying ordeal nearly killed the rabbi. A few days later, on *Rosh Hashanah*, he had himself carried to the synagogue in his coffin next to his severed limbs. As

---

[4] Translator's note: *Mayence*: Former English name (and current French name) of the city of Mainz.

[5] Translator's note: This legendary rabbi is said to have lived in the tenth and eleventh centuries, not the sixteenth. In some versions of the story, it is an archbishop who pressures him to convert to Christianity. Medieval legend says that Rabbi Amnon wrote this well-known liturgical poem, the *Unetanneh Tokef*. Evidence suggests, though, that it is an ancient Middle Eastern composition.

the *hazzan* was about to recite the *Kedushah*, Rabbi Amnon interrupted and improvised this eloquent prayer that Jews still recite today in all their houses of worship:

I will declare the mighty holiness of this day, for it is awful and tremendous. Thy kingdom is exalted thereon. Thou art the Judge, and at the same time, accuser and witness. Thou writest, sealest, recordest and remembrest all our deeds. And when the great trumpet of judgment is sounded, even the angels are terrified, for before Thy supreme purity, the angels themselves are not faultless. All who have entered the world pass before Thee, even as the shepherd causes the flock he numbers to pass under his crook. On the New Year it is written, and on the Day of Atonement each human destiny is sealed; but penitence, prayer and charity, O Lord, may avert all evil decrees. Thy wrath is slow to ignite and swift to wane. Thou dost not wish the death of Thy creature; Thou seest the strength of his passions, and Thou knowest that man is made of flesh and blood. Perishable man, who cometh from dust, is like a fragile vase, like dried grass, like a withered flower, like a fleeting shadow, like a vanishing mist, like the wind that blows; he dissipateth like the dust and disappeareth like a dream. But Thou, King of the Universe, Thou art all-powerful and eternal. Thy years are countless, the number of Thy days is infinite; the mystery of Thy name is impenetrable. Thy name is worthy of Thee, and Thou art worthy of Thy name. Act, then, for Thine own name's sake, and glorify Thy name with those who glorify it.[6]

---

[6] Translator's note: The English here is adapted in part from p. 229 of *The Talmud: Selections*, translated by H. Polano (1876).

Rosh Hashanah lasts two days, with the same prayers and rites on both days. Both afternoons around two o'clock, the youths of the village gather again at synagogue to recite the most beautiful Psalms of David together. Some years they perform this act of piety with special fervor. This happens if, in the morning, despite the pious *shofar* blower's skill, the horn did not make all the sounds as cleanly and crisply as usual. That is a bad sign for the coming year, and no matter how fervently they pray to God that afternoon, it is sometimes not possible to deflect the sinister omen: The year was 1807, and in those days Reb Auscher blew the *shofar* in Wintzenheim. In vain, the rabbi had said loudly and clearly as usual, "*Tekiah, shevorim, teruah!*" Reb Auscher blew into the ram's horn as hard as he could, but all that came out were strange, truncated squawks. That afternoon, the whole *kehillah* (congregation) prayed for Heaven to deflect the omen. Heavenly decrees are often inscrutable, though. Six months later, surely in atonement for unknown sins, two-thirds of the congregation died in an epidemic of which Wintzenheim still retains tragic memories.

After the *Rosh Hashanah* celebrations, I could not dream of leaving Wintzenheim before the *Yom Kippur* observance, only ten days after the New Year's ceremonies. In ancient Judea when Israel was a nation, Jews celebrated *Yom Kippur* in Jerusalem with unparalleled formality. When the populace gathered in the forecourt of the Temple, the high priest made the usual burnt offerings. Then the two expiatory goats were brought to him.

The blood of one, intended for Jehovah, bathed the altars of the Temple; the other, whose name has become proverbial, was the *scapegoat*. The high priest would place his hands on it and, confessing the sins of Israel, he would symbolically transfer everyone's iniquities to the goat and send it into the desert. The high priest then entered the *Holy of Holies* and implored God's forgiveness for the people kneeling within the Temple walls. Such was the ancient *Yom Kippur*. The ceremony bearing that name among today's Jews has lost none of its original majesty: for Jewish communities, the day remains singularly austere, religious and serious.[7] In this humble village of Wintzenheim, no household failed to prepare for it devoutly. Villagers whose work usually kept them in the mountains or in the neighboring Munster Valley had returned to pray with their families. A strange spectacle, this lasting influence of ancient traditions in a race that so many people think worships nothing but material possessions!

In every home on the day before *Yom Kippur*, the *kapporah* ceremony occurs. On a bare table set up in the middle of the main room, a prayer book sits open to a passage marked in advance. Roosters and hens lie tied up on the floor. The head of the family comes forward, unties the legs of one rooster, picks it up and reads the ceremonial prayer from the book. At a certain moment in the prayer, he lifts the rooster, swings it in three circles

---

[7] Even in Paris, this holiday is celebrated with special reverence. A Jewish family occupying one of the highest financial positions in Europe is known for its zealous observance of *Yom Kippur* in all its severity.

over his head and repeats aloud: "Be my redemption for what would rightly befall me. To redeem my sins, this rooster shall go to death." Everyone present does the same in turn. The hens are reserved for women while roosters represent the ransom of men. Once the *kapporah* is done, the roosters and hens—clearly echoing the scapegoat of old Jerusalem—are sent to the sacrificer[8] who alone is qualified to kill them according to ritual, which means cutting their windpipe.

It says in Deuteronomy, "Then shall it be, if the guilty man deserve to be beaten, that the judge shall cause him to lie down, and to be beaten before his face, according to the degree of his fault, by a certain number. Forty stripes may he give him." The day before *Yom Kippur*, this prescription from Deuteronomy has symbolic application. The men alone go to synagogue around one in the afternoon in everyday clothes. After reciting a prayer, they pair up: one lies on the floor and the other, standing with a long leather strap in his hand, lashes him with it softly. Each time the strap strikes him, the prostrate man beats his breast.[9] Once each pair has complied with this Biblical decree, they go home and will return in the evening. The synagogue is magnificently illuminated by then. The men have brought the linen tunic that will serve as their shroud, which every good Jew prepares well in advance. At the service, they wear this tunic—their future grave clothes—and hide their head under the folds of the holy

---

[8] The *hazzan* generally does this duty.

[9] Typically thirty-nine lashes: that is the number now established by the rabbis.

Kapporah.

tallith.[10] They will do the same all the next day. For three hours, one prayer follows another as the *hazzan* and congregation respond to each other out loud. Only after nightfall do they disperse.

One more word about the eve of *Yom Kippur*, a mysterious night if ever there was one, when strange occurrences are often observed. That night, long after the faithful return home, the deceased make their own procession to the synagogue. Dressed in shrouds, the local dead will address their prayers to the God of Israel. Usually around midnight, without anyone hearing their movements or footsteps, they advance towards the tabernacle by the light of the eternal lamp. They open the Holy Ark, remove a *Torah* scroll and place it on the sacred platform. Then one of them starts reading the paragraphs of the *Torah* chapter that the *hazzan* will chant to the faithful the next day on *Yom Kippur*. Before each paragraph, the *hazzan* of the dead utters the name of a living member of the community. And pity the person whose name was uttered that night in front of that funereal congregation! In Fegersheim, Jews still tell the story of what happened to Reb Salme Baumblatt, the village's *shofar* blower, on *Yom Kippur* Eve in 1780. He had stayed late visiting his daughter, who had given birth and was ill. Now to get home he had to pass the synagogue. It was almost midnight when he rounded the corner of the sacred building. Suddenly, he distinctly heard these words: *Salme Baumblatt!* He shuddered and replied calmly, "Already?"

---

[10] A sort of head shawl worn during prayer.

The great atonement.

"Sorle," he told his wife when he got home, "tomorrow, after *Yom Kippur*, there's no point putting away my *kittel* (shroud), for I will need it soon." The incredulous Sorle began to laugh.

"Laugh away," her husband answered. "I know what I'm talking about."

Alas, the poor woman's laughter turned quickly to tears. Three days after that exchange, they carried Salme Baumblatt to the Fegersheim cemetery.

Daylight, however, ends the service of the dead and brings in the living, who will not leave the synagogue until after sundown. This day is *Yom Kippur* proper. No one wears shoes. Some congregants push devotion to the point of never sitting during this long service. Four times, the people confess and prostrate themselves. Each confession, which God alone receives, is preceded by prayers written by great religious scholars. Some are of truly rare eloquence, including the one authored by Rabbi Samtob ben Adontiat that introduces the great morning prayer.[11]

> Sovereign of the Universe! When I behold the luster of my youth vanished; and the creatures of my imagination, all of them, fled as a shadow; my sins are as red as scarlet... I must almost despair of curing my backslidings, or making effica-

---

[11] A rabbi of the Spanish school who flourished in Leon in the first half of the fourteenth century. [Translator's note: A reference to the medieval Spanish Jewish poet Santob de Carrión, who might or might not have been a rabbi. The author found these passages in one of the few High Holiday prayer books available in French at the time: a "Spanish-rite" (Sephardic) volume. This prayer is not usually said in Ashkenazic synagogues, such as those in 19th-century Alsace.]

cious repentance, since the day is so short, and the labor so great... Yet how exceeding precious is redemption; and how shall I, poor and destitute of good works, obtain acquittal? Therefore is my head bent down as a bulrush; and my tears, reddened with my liver's blood, flow copiously, like the scattering of dill and cumin seed. But, verily, my reins reprove me, and my thoughts encourage and strengthen me; by saying to me, "Hasten to implore redemption, for the day still lingers; and although the Judge be awful and tremendous, yet despair not of obtaining mercy; the sun is yet above the horizon, and hasteneth not to go down till the day be over. Persevere till there is room for thy cry, and a door opened to thy prayer..."

No less beautiful is the prayer that precedes the afternoon's great confession. It is the work of Rabbi Isaac ben Israel.[12] How well it responds to the repentance and contrition of the whole congregation!

Sovereign of the Universe, at the time of offering the evening sacrifice, when I reflect on my sin, fear and dread seize me. I am struck with astonishment when I reflect that God will rise up in judgment. When He demandeth an account, what answer shall I return Him? What can one composed of the dust of the earth answer in the presence of Him who dwelleth on high? I have earnestly desired an advocate to plead in my behalf; I have searched within myself for him, but could not find him. I made application to my head, fore-

---

[12] He lived in Toledo, Spain, in the late thirteenth century.

head and face, to intercede for me before the Lord. But my head answered me, "How dare that head lift up itself, which hath behaved with such levity?" My face replied, "Wherewith wilt thou reconcile thyself unto the Lord—the wicked man who hast hardened thy face?" My forehead also answered me, saying, "O how canst thou be justified, who art born of a woman, and thy sin is engraven upon thy heart, and thy forehead is so brazen?"

Between the *Mincha* (afternoon) prayer and the *Nehillah* (closing) prayer comes an ancient and moving ceremony: the blessing of the people by descendants of the family of Aaron. The ritual occurs almost exactly as it did long ago at this season at the Temple in Jerusalem. In every Jewish community, some families have retained the name of *Cohen* or *Cohanim*[13] as descendants of Aaron, and others the name *Levi*, as descendants of that tribe. The Levites, as we know, were servants to the priestly family. So on *Yom Kippur*, around half past three, the *Levis* in the congregation walked towards the Holy Ark. One of them held a ewer filled with water in one hand and a basin in the other. They were then approached by the *Cohanim* in the congregation. Each *Levi* poured water alternatively over the two hands of each *Cohen*. In ancient times, this is how the Levites used to serve and aid the priests in their religious duties. The *Levis* now returned to their places. The *Cohanim*, thus purified, slowly climbed the steps to the Ark. Suddenly, the *hazzan* called

---

[13] *Cohen* in Hebrew means "priest."

to the *Cohanim*. After covering their heads with the *tallith*, they turned towards the congregation, who lowered their eyes. Indeed, no one may look at the *Cohanim* at that moment just as no one may look at a *shofar* blower on *Rosh Hashanah*, for the divine spirit hovers over the *shofar* blower's head then just as it now radiates from the brow of the Aaronites. Spreading each hand so that three fingers were on one side and two on the other, they extended them towards the congregation. In chorus, to a traditional melody, they chanted the same benediction that God dictated to Moses to be taught to the Aaronites. The priests of old gave this same blessing to the people in the time of the Temple: "The Lord bless and preserve thee! The Lord make his face to shine upon thee, and be gracious unto thee! The Lord lift up his countenance upon thee, and give thee peace!"

Yom Kippur ends with the recitation of a touching prayer, the *Nehillah* or closing prayer as the Hebrew word indicates. The wax tapers burning since the previous day make distinctive crackling sounds at that moment, as if showing fatigue. Their glimmer illuminates that whole congregation dressed in white, fasting, contrite. In an instant, God will seal His judgments irrevocably. Even as they plead to Him! Did He not say that He seeks not the death of the sinner? "Behold! Behold this people, repentant and confessed. God shall inscribe His people in the book of life."

So prayed the faithful. The first shadows of night were already invading the room. As the final act of the great day, the *hazzan*, amid universal silence, proclaims the ancient dogma of the oneness of God, which is like the watchword of the Jewish people: "Hear, O Israel, the Lord is our God, the Lord is one."[14] The people repeat this verse seven times with enthusiastic conviction. Next the *shofar* sounds to announce the close of this impressive ceremony, and everyone leaves in silence.

---

[14] These are the words that Jews are asked to repeat when dying. The great tragic actress Mademoiselle Rachel died reciting them.

CHAPTER FOUR

*The Feast of Booths; their origin and dual nature. —
The sukkah and its decoration. — The great
Hosanna. — Papa Nadel and his family. — The first
day of Chol Hamoed. — A matrimonial meeting. —
Jewish betrothals. — An important personage. — The
betrothal dinner; folk songs. — A lustik. —
Conclusion.*

AUTUMN IS THE SEASON when Jewish holidays are
most plentiful. September had returned with its cool,
misty mornings and longer evenings, and I had not left
Alsace. I was in Hegenheim, a village on the Swiss border
just one league from Basle. There I would celebrate a holiday that had given me the loveliest memories ever since
childhood: *Sukkoth*, also called the *Feast of Tabernacles*
or of *Booths*. Hegenheim has had a large Jewish population since time immemorial, made up of cattle mer-
chants, peddlers and clockmakers who all do business in
and with Switzerland. A kind and honest clockmaker
friend of Papa Salomon's, little Aron, had offered me his
hospitality. I arrived at his home as promised, the day
before the holiday (September 22).

For the ancient Israelites, *Sukkoth* had both agricultural and historical meaning. Agriculturally, it marked
the end of the harvests, the gathering of all the fruit of

the trees and the vine. Also, presumably as a symbol of the harvest, the Law required people to bring a bundle of several plants to the Temple on the first day of the holiday. Historically, *Sukkoth* commemorates the Israelites' wanderings in the desert, in memory of which they must live in temporary dwellings for seven days each year at this season. Hence *Feast of Tabernacles* or *Booths*.

All of this is obeyed rigorously in our countryside. Three days before the holiday, everywhere in the village, such bustle and activity! Men, lads and little boys all work on the *sukkah* or booth. In every courtyard, on every corner, in every little square, they build rustic shelters for themselves and their whole family. The foundations of these outdoor huts are four solid posts sunk deep into the ground. Staggered between these are poles that serve as the booth's walls. The outside of each wall is covered in foliage and moss while on the inside, to block the wind, wide hangings of white fabric flutter to the ground on every side. The ceiling is a wooden trellis covered in fir branches laid in every direction, cut from neighboring forests. Local peasants, who know the Jewish calendar wonderfully well, have been coming to the hamlets every morning for days to supply the markets with these branches. The huts' ceiling decoration is a matter of firm tradition. Chains of blue and yellow paper hang like drapes alongside wild rose branches with red hips, an attractive contrast to the greenery. Attached to the trellis are all the fruits of the season: pears, apples, grapes, nuts. Finally, dangling majestically not far from the door is an essential, infallible protection against all evil influences:

a glorious red onion with rooster feathers sticking out of it as ornaments. No Alsatian Jew can remember any malign spirit, no matter how malicious it was, successfully intruding by day or night into a *sukkah* furnished with that precious bulb. In the middle of the ceiling, as close to the trellis as the other ornaments, triangles of gilded rods form the classic Star of David (*mogen Doved*), through which hangs a notched extender holding the seven-spouted lamp. Sometimes it rains but this frail structure is ready for anything: the removable doors can double as a roof. On rainy evenings, we huddle together even more happily in the improvised shelter amid the penetrating scent of fir trees. It is lovely to hear the rain on the *sukkah*'s greenery, adornments and coverings, as the flickering lamp lights a table laid with Alsatian abundance.

I recall that another *Sukkoth* guest was expected at my host's home in Hegenheim: Papa Salomon's fine son Shemele, and we all knew that the holiday was not the only reason for his journey. He was there to continue a marriage negotiation begun by the *shadshen* Ephraim Schwab. Shemele and Deborah, the daughter of wealthy Nadel, were to meet for the first time. If they liked each other, I could count on the curious spectacle of a traditional Alsatian Jewish betrothal ceremony.

The synagogue's annual *Sukkoth* services have the same rustic tone as the joyous family gatherings in the *sukkahs*. The faithful arrive there in the morning. In their left hand, they carry a small basket or golden box containing a citron, and in their right hand, a long palm

The *sukkah*.

branch (*lulef*) to which a bouquet of myrtle is attached. This is all meant to evoke the holiday's pastoral side. A vital moment in the ceremony comes after the *hazzan* (prayer leader) proclaims God's bounty: all the congregants reply with a solemn *Hosanna* and walk throughout the synagogue shaking the palm branches, which strike each other audibly and release a wild aroma I cannot identify, redolent of the East.

On the first afternoon of the holiday, we followed custom and went visiting. First, Aron took me to Papa Nadel's *sukkah*, which truly was a model booth. White and pink flowers spelled out this Bible verse about the holiday in Hebrew letters on each inner wall: "In booths shall ye dwell seven days." Inside the shelter, seated royally between his wife and daughter, Papa Nadel was holding court.

He exclaimed as we entered, "Gentlemen, have a seat. There's room here for everyone. Deborah, some glasses, some biscuits, some wine for these gentlemen!"

I looked at the young woman, who served us with graceful, gracious agility. Ephraim Schwab was right: Deborah was beautiful. Such eyes, such a dazzling complexion, but most of all, such hair! This was Jewish hair in all its gorgeous luxuriance. Although the teeth of a huge comb bit it down firmly, her mane always seemed about to escape and tumble down.

"Fradel," said Papa Nadel to his wife, introducing us. "This is the man I told you about, a friend of the Salomon family."

Deborah blushed slightly.

The *lulef*.

"To your health, gentlemen! Today is *yontof* (a holy day). Try some of this red wine. And there's better wine to come. Isn't there, Fradel? Isn't there, Deborah? I have a special straw wine that you'll drink later…"

"The day after tomorrow maybe," Aron added mischievously.

"Uh-uh!" said Nadel in a serious tone.

"Yes, be quiet," cut in the lady of the house. "Who knows the future? Sometimes…"

"Go on!" replied Aron. "Take it from me, the day after tomorrow, we'll be *breaking the cup*."

Deborah smiled now.

The conversation ended abruptly as a stream of visitors arrived in holiday finery. We ceded our space to the newcomers and continued our tour, as one does on *yontof*.

The first day of *Chol Hamoed* (the semi-holy days) arrived. This was the very day when my friend Shemele was expected at Aron's. The weather was beautiful. A good autumnal sun shone on the horizon. The village was lively. Vehicles came and went, crowded with passengers. These were, as they say in the country, *Chol Hamoed people*, some going to neighboring villages and others coming to visit Hegenheim. Leisurely groups strolled or sat on wooden beams in the street to chat. It was around one o'clock. We had just had lunch in Aron's *sukkah*. Far off, we heard a vehicle approaching and soon saw a yellow *char-à-bancs* drawn by a small gray horse. It stopped at Aron's house. Before the young driver even had time to climb down, my host's son rushed to meet him. The new arrival was none other than the son of my old friend

Salomon, the elegant Shemele. By a marked coincidence, the young man had barely entered the festive home and returned his hosts' warm greetings when another figure, also expected in Hegenheim, presented himself. This was a man in his mid sixties. He wore an otterskin cap, green frock coat, short breeches and yellow turned-down boots. He was covered in dust.

"Well, then!" he cried out when he spotted Shemele, who was still brushing himself off. "You didn't beat me here by much!"

The respected matchmaker Ephraim Schwab was right on time as well.

Meanwhile, it must be said, the whole Nadel household was preparing for battle.

Ephraim Schwab went there first on his own. He entered with a familiarity granted by the importance of his mission. He dropped into an armchair, crossed his legs, wiped his brow, gave a hearty cough and blew his nose loudly. He had to be shown to his room and to the lavabo in the hallway where he could wash his hands before eating and drinking, as tradition requires. After consuming food and drink, he began to praise Salomon and Shemele. This was natural.

In the meantime, Aron and Shemele entered the house. The pretense, of course, was that Shemele was making a simple social call: he would not have gone to Hegenheim without paying his respects to Nadel and his family, and he hoped that when Nadel went to Mulhouse, he would return the favor and visit Papa Salomon. This common ruse avoids the awkwardness of a formal marriage interview in case either party is not interested. They talked of business, news, religious holidays. Deborah paid close attention, and Shemele, still conversing, kept gazing at her. She joined the discussion twice and he found her a good conversationalist. For her part, the lovely Deborah listened to the inexhaustible Shemele with visible interest. Yes, Lazare the beggar had been right when he said, "Shemele is not one to be embarrassed when courting a girl or her parents." The lad now proved it clearly. Moments later, the two women went out for a moment and returned carrying plates loaded with all types of sweets. The mother poured a liqueur into little glasses and Deborah did the honors.

"How long do you plan to stay in Hegenheim?" Nadel asked Shemele.

"I'm so happy right here that I'm not eager to leave," replied Shemele.

Papa Nadel exchanged glances with his wife and daughter to get their opinion, and then said, "The longer you stay with us, Mr. Shemele, the happier we will be."

Reading between the lines, this meant they had reached an agreement.

We went back to Aron's and that night during dinner, Papa Nadel and his wife came to invite Shemele and the rest of us for supper the next evening, Thursday. This meant "Tomorrow evening is the betrothal." Shemele sent a letter by messenger. The next day at noon, Papa Salomon and his wife arrived at a jog trot in a pretty *char-à-bancs* they had rented. They climbed down and made straight for the Nadel home.

Now the great trumpet of Common Knowledge—in the form of Mr. Baer, teacher at the Jewish primary school—announced from house to house that pretty Deborah would be betrothed to Shemele, son of *Salomon-Bollwiller*.

The betrothal would be that evening, on the second day of *Chol Hamoed*.

I made a point to stay in Hegenheim for the ceremony, which they celebrated with that scrupulous respect for tradition typical of all Jewish villages in Alsace.

Since morning, the Nadels' kitchen had been under the command of the great Dina, Hegenheim's first cordon-bleu chef. The clamor of geese and chickens to be massacred that day mingled with the clinking of a brass mortar, in which much sugar and cinnamon was being ground for pastries. The house exhaled delicious aromas, and passersby on their way from synagogue said, "You can smell the *knasmal* (betrothal meal)."

Starting at six, the Nadels' most beautiful room welcomed the main guests. A chintz tablecloth covered a round table in the middle of the floor. The gathering included Nadel and his wife as well as Papa Salomon, kindly Yedele, Aron, and all their loved ones. Shemele and Deborah sat close together and talked softly. They often looked at each other in mutual satisfaction without speaking, and then continued chatting. Ephraim Schwab went back and forth, offering everyone a pinch from his ample snuffbox. Soon a tide of neighbors and friends rolled in, followed by prominent figures whose presence on such occasions is obligatory: the rabbi, the *hazzan*, the *shammes* (the synagogue's beadle) and the schoolteacher.

Only one person was missing, and he did not keep us waiting long. A man entered, not without first kissing the *mezuzah*[1] attached to the doorframe. This fellow, whose hat rested on the back of his neck to form a magnificent obtuse angle with the rest of his body, wore a long gray frock coat, a floral-patterned large under-waistcoat, and thoroughly short trousers that revealed blue striped stockings. A very narrow clipped white beard framed his face starting at the temples, in keeping with the casuistic interpretation of this article of Mosaic Law: "Ye shall not cut round the corners of the hair of your head, neither shalt thou destroy the corners of thy beard."[2] The new arrival approached the master and mistress of the house first, and then the Salomon family. He greeted Papa Salomon with the usual "*Sholem aleichem*," and merely nodded to the others present, who were all locals. Then he sat at the round table in the middle of the room, on which an inkstand stood next to a quire of paper. What was this man? He was Reb Lippmann, but let us explain further. Reb Lippmann, as the *Reb* before his name indicates, is a qualified Talmudic scholar, as exist in so many of our villages. His work, already alluded to, is this: Each morning starting at ten, he goes to say his *shier* (prayer of

---

[1] A tinplate case attached to a doorpost. Written on parchment inside it is the Jews' most important prayer, which begins with these sacramental words: *Hear, O Israel, the Lord our God is one.*

[2] Leviticus 19:27.

blessing)[3] in a good number of affluent homes. He has his subscribers. He also says prayers in houses of mourning for the deceased to rest in peace. He prepares boys for their religious initiation. He composes Hebrew inscriptions for gravestones. It is he who knows how to attach the myrtle and willow branches to the bottom of the *lulef* that people shake during *Sukkoth*, combining them artfully while complying with the rules of *din* (custom). Is a villager so sick that doctors have given him up for dead? At the family's expense, Reb Lippmann will travel by foot to the grand duchy of Hesse-Darmstadt, to Michelstadt, where Rabbi Saekel the Kabbalist lives. The venerable rabbi gives him all kinds of charms that Reb Lippmann brings to the sick. The charms rarely fail.

Lastly, versatile Reb Lippmann is also responsible for drawing up marriage agreements in the desired form. The document specifies the size of the dowry, what gifts the couple intend to exchange, and how long after the betrothal the wedding will occur, usually one year.

After writing at length in ponderous silence, Reb Lippman stood and proclaimed the content of the *tenoim* (marriage agreement). The wedding would be in six months. Reb Lippmann had resisted talk of such a short engagement at first but Shemele, through his father, was so insistent that Reb Lippmann had to admit his own misjudgment.

Then came the symbolic act of betrothal. Reb Lippmann took a piece of chalk from the immense pocket of

[3] Translator's note: In fact, a *shier* is not a prayer but a Talmudic lesson.

his under-waistcoat. He drew a chalk circle in the center of the room and had everyone move into it, with Shemele facing Deborah. Reb Lippmann, at the center of the group, held out a portion of his coat to each witness, and they all touched it in succession. Then he went to the chest of drawers, took a cup placed there for this purpose, and returned to his place amid the others, still in a circle. He raised an arm—to strengthen the momentum, no doubt—and dropped the cup, which broke into a thousand bits. Reb Lippmann shouted, *"Mazel tof!"* Everyone repeated in chorus, *"Mazel tof!"* and each of them picked up a piece of the shattered cup to take away. The couple was now betrothed. The chalk circle means the bridegroom and the bride must never stray from the line they have entered. Under Talmudic law, everyone touching the garment is a sign of assent in every possible type of transaction. The broken cup, like the bottle broken on a wedding day, is a sort of *memento mori* in action: there is no joy without sorrow. In any case, *mazel tof* is a common Hebrew phrase of congratulations that means, roughly, "May everything be for the best."

Moments after the ceremony, Papa Nadel and Papa Salomon shepherded Ephraim into an adjacent room. Through the door, we heard metallic clinking. As per custom, they immediately paid the fees of the *shadshen* (matchmaker). Ephraim Schwab charged the usual amount: 4 percent of the dowry. He reemerged beaming.

The betrothal meal began, and went happily on and on amid universal praise for the great Dina's culinary talent. Nadel, as promised, introduced us to his straw wine, which lived up to its reputation. During dessert, I had another chance to witness some of these traditions that Jews have always revered. This is the moment in the meal when betrothal gifts are exchanged. Salomon gave a box to his son, who handed it to his fiancée: it contained a brooch and a gold belt buckle. Nadel, in turn, took a sha-green leather case from his pocket and passed it to Shemele. The case held a magnificent meerschaum pipe with metal trim and a lid, with a little silver chain. Then the synagogue's *hazzan* was introduced with his two as-sistants: a tenor and bass whose voices would accompany him.[4]

The *hazzan* sang a blessing for the future couple. That was the signal for a short concert in which the teacher, Mr. Baer, soon played the principal role. People begged him for some of the beloved old folk tunes of Jewish Al-sace. Without holding out too long, Monsieur Baer launched into one of those songs whose plaintive, serious melody is so typical. It began with the story of creation, followed by the sin of our first ancestors.

"When God made the world, all was darkness and night; no sun, no moon, no stars." And a bit later: "The wily serpent slithered towards Eve and said mysteriously, 'Both you and Adam are to be pitied, for you are forbid-den to eat this fruit (the apple)! The apple, I tell you, has a wondrous property: anyone who tastes it will be en-dowed with divine power. Believe me, eat one."

[4] These three form the synagogue's vocal orchestra. The *hazzan* is an important, well-paid personage. Assistant *hazzans* earn a pittance but may practice other trades. You can often find them competing with the village barber or schoolteacher.

Then came the song called the *"Kalleh-Lid"* (bride's song), describing the future wife's duties. The lyric's humble exterior—like all the rest, it is just rhymed German prose—hides a profound moral. I always become emotional when I hear the tender, sad tune that accompanies these words:

> Listen, good people, to how things should be done among the Children of Israel. Young woman: However virtuous you may have been, you might also have made mistakes. Even as you step under the *chuppah* (wedding canopy), you should lament, weep, and ask forgiveness from your father and mother. Be charitable always, for God is the friend of the needy. Does a poor person come knocking at your door? Answer and ease his misery. God will reward you: you will be rich and happy and will give birth without pain.

The teacher's performance of popular Jewish Alsatian tunes concluded with the famous song "Moses the Prophet."[5]

> Who in the whole universe can be compared to Moshe (Moses)? Did God not meet with him in his own tent, face to face? And therefore he had to die. When Moshe's days reached their end, God said to him, "Your time is come, you will go the way of all mortals." "Alas!" replied Moshe, "I shall

---

[5] We give it here in slightly altered form, as we have filled in gaps with a poetic legend from the *Midrash*, published by our learned friend S. Munk in his article "De la poésie hébraïque après la Bible," as an insert in the newspaper *Le Temps* on December 27, 1834.

not be allowed to tread the sacred soil of the Promised Land!" And he rent his garments, covered himself in ashes and began to pray. His prayer shook the heavens and the earth and all of creation. But the Lord ordered His angels to close Heaven's gate to Moshe's prayer, for the prayers of the just can penetrate like the blade of a sword, and nothing can resist them: "Lord," said Moshe again. "You know everything I suffered for revealing your name to Israel and teaching them your Laws. I was a faithful guide for your people in days of tribulation, and now that everything smiles upon them, you forbid me to pass the banks of the Yarden (Jordan) with them." "Enough," said the Lord. "The ruling is pronounced and nothing can reverse it." The man of God had just enough time to write his final canticle to Israel, for he had barely finished it when the fatal moment came. The Lord ordered Gabriel to bring Him Moshe's soul. The archangel asked, "How could I watch the death of this holy man who, by himself, is worth as much as the sixty myriads of Israel?" And the Lord said unto Michael, "Go bring me the soul of Moshe." "Lord," said Michael. "I was his teacher, he was my disciple, so I cannot watch him die."

Then came the *Malech Hamovess* (Angel of Death), who cuts off the days of all descendants of Adam. He had long counted the hours and minutes, rejoicing in the approaching death of this man of God. "Go," says the Lord, "and fetch me the soul of Moshe, son of Amram." The *Malech Hamovess* girds himself with cruelty, wraps himself in rage, and hurls himself to Earth. On his sword, three drops of strychnine glisten. He approaches Moshe, who was still writing his canticle and was inscribing the ineffable name of the Deity. Upon seeing Moshe's face shine like the sun, the *Malech Hamovess* was seized with terror. He dropped his sword and fled trembling. Then a celestial voice rang out: "Moshe," it said, "the time is come." Moshe began to weep from the depths of his heart. "Lord!" he cried. "Deliver me not unto the exterminating angel!" "Fear nothing," replied the same voice. "And make haste."

Moshe sanctified himself again with ardent prayers, and God Himself descended from on high in all His glory. The three archangels flew behind him and gathered around Moshe's bed. And the Lord said unto Moshe's soul, "My daughter, I fixed a time of one hundred twenty years for you to dwell in the body of Moshe; that time is past, so go out and come rise to the heavens, where I shall place you beneath my throne, next to cherubim and seraphim..." And then God embraced Moshe and took his soul with a kiss, and God Himself wept for him. Four archangels, with veiled face, then carried him through the air in a coffin. God purified the body in flame and then lifted it in His own arms, and no one in Israel has ever discovered where the grave lies.

This rather stark poetry inspired a sort of pensiveness among the guests, bordering on sadness. Fortunately, at such events and other Alsatian gatherings, there are always skilled *lustiks* who can unfurrow the most somber brows. One merry guest excelled at imitating all kinds of animal sounds. We heard him neigh like a horse, meow like a cat, bark like a dog, crow like a rooster. That is all it took to entertain the guests, and the meal ended as it began, amid frank hilarity.

I could thus observe the distinctive traits of a rather frequent facet of *Sukkoth*. These days of rest and blissful gaiety are the easiest time of year for Jews to form those first bonds, those graceful preludes to marriage called betrothals. The traditional ceremony blends so harmoniously with the vibrant spectacle of our communities on that holiday, when villages become rustic campsites heady with the scent of pine that wafts in like a breath of youth and springtime. What I have told you about the inner world of the Salomon and Nadel families is a fair prediction of what Shemele and Deborah's life will be like, now and in the future. It will be a mix of work and peaceful domestic joys, brightened here and there by the religious holidays that punctuate life in Jewish villages. My memory of these celebrations, so impressive in their simple originality, is the main thing I took with me when I set out from Hegenheim. I confess I left with some regret. Entering Paris, I thought of the beautiful poem at the start of Goethe's *Divan*, and told myself that it is sweet sometimes, amid our troubled and hectic lives, to go pay our respects to the land of the patriarchs, and in the heart of Europe, breathe the air of the ancient Orient.

Evening prayer.

PART III:

WINTER JEWISH
HOLIDAYS

CHAPTER ONE

Purim, or the Jewish carnival. — Its historical origin. — The book of Esther, or Megillah. — Purim in Alsace. — The fast known as the fast of Esther. — The Megillah reading. — Characteristic incidents and details. — Hammers. — Purim morning. — Afternoon; shlach moness. — Supper. — A required dish. — The usual guests. — Costumes. — Two plays.

FOR COMPLETENESS, I SHALL round out these rural sketches by introducing the reader to two more Jewish holidays that are less solemn, less serious and much less important than the ones already described. These two festivals are seldom if ever celebrated in big cities nowadays. They are interesting, though, less for their origin than for the thoroughly Biblical way that devout Alsatian country people observe them.

One of these holidays comes in late winter, and the other near the start of that season. We shall begin with memories of the first: the joyous festival of *Purim* or carnival. To be clear and avoid confusion, though, there is carnival and there is carnival. The Jews' *Purim* has absolutely nothing in common with the Christian carnival. The latter, you know, is basically an echo of the Greek Lupercalia and Roman Saturnalia, tempered by the modern spirit. The Christian carnival is a time of exuberant delight and wildness, permitted in supposed compensation for the asceticism of Lent. These delights and this wildness peak in the three days before the mournful observance of Ash Wednesday.

Our *Purim* has a completely different origin and purpose. *Purim* marks the anniversary of the Jews' deliverance during the reign of Ahasuerus. That happened when beautiful, virtuous Esther overcame the bloody royal edict that cruel Haman had obtained against all the Jews of Persia. Ever since their captivity, Jews had been spread throughout the vast empire of the Persian monarchs who succeeded the kings of Babylon.

We all know of this event thanks to the book of Esther and because of Racine's immortal verse drama based on the Bible account. Let us summarize and examine the story a bit, looking step by step at this chronicle that is still known in Jewish ritual as the *Megillah*, and let us see what it teaches us.

The king's new all-powerful advisor, Haman the Amalekite, could not forgive Mordecai the Jew (noble son of the tribe of Benjamin) for his contempt and scorn towards Haman. The upstart vizier went to the king and slandered the Jews, his new subjects, and gained permission to have them slaughtered throughout the empire on a given date. However, Mordecai's adopted daughter, Esther, had replaced proud Queen Vashti on the throne. The king loved Esther tenderly though he did not yet know her religion.

When Mordecai ascertained all that had been done, Mordecai rent his clothes, put on sackcloth strewed with ashes, and went out into the midst of the city, and cried with a loud and bitter cry.

And thus he came up to the front of the king's gate; for none dared to enter into the king's gate clothed with sackcloth.

And Mordecai sent word unto Esther of all that had happened, and a copy of the law that had been given out at Shushan to destroy the Jews, and charged her that she should go in unto the king to make supplication unto him, and to request mercy for her people.

On pain of death, no one could approach the king without being summoned first, unless he showed mercy by immediately holding out his scepter towards the intruder. So Esther hesitated, but Mordecai convinced her she must risk everything to save her people:

Then Esther sent this answer back to Mordecai: Go, assemble together all the Jews who are now present in Shushan, and fast ye for me...; also I myself with my maidens will fast in like manner; and then will I go in unto the king; and if I then perish, I perish.

Esther appeared before the king and found favor in his eyes. She told him all and unmasked Haman's evil plot. The king had his vizier hanged from the same gallows that Haman had prepared for Mordecai, and the terrible edict was revoked.

> Then were called the king's scribes; and they wrote all Mordecai's commands to the Jews, and to the lieutenants and the governors of the 127 provinces of the empire, unto every people according to its language, and to the Jews according to their tongue. All was written and sealed in the name of the king, and was sent through means of the swift messengers on horseback, and riders on mules and camels.

The stay of execution arrived everywhere in time. On the fourteenth day of the twelfth month—the month of *Adar* (February–March)—on the date the executions were to have happened:

> The Jews made a feast day with lights and entertainment and joy, and of sending portions one to the other, and gifts to the needy. Because Haman the son of Hammedatha, the Agagite, the adversary of all the Jews, had devised against the Jews to exterminate them, and had cast the *Pur*, that is, the lot, to choose the day on which to destroy them... Therefore did they call these days *Purim*.

It is easy to see why some people call *Purim* "carnival" despite the differences. The comparison is meant to suggest all the joy and merry-making of the Jewish *Purim*.

We are now in our Alsatian villages and today is the 14th of the month of *Adar*: the day before *Purim*. Every man, woman and child in the community is fasting in memory of the fast that the Jews of Shushan undertook with Mordecai and Esther, while the Jewess-turned-queen prepared to seek a favorable audience with stern Ahasuerus. Fortunately for our fasting villagers, the daylight hours on the 14th of *Adar* (which falls in late February or early March) are reasonably short. Jews therefore extend the fast slightly and do not break it until one hour past sundown. Why? Because *Purim* begins with a public reading of the book of Esther in the synagogue, which cannot begin until daylight vanishes completely, and the reading lasts at least a full hour. We enter the synagogue. The whole *kehillah* (community) is gathered. Wax tapers known as *Purim candles* light the holy building. The men stand behind little desks and the women are in a gallery reserved for them. All the boys in the *kehillah* arrange themselves in view of their parents, holding superb, freshly fashioned wooden hammers. In front of the *hazzan* on the sacred platform sits a parchment scroll that the *shammes* will unroll as the *hazzan* reads it. Handwritten on this parchment is the book of Esther, also called the *Megillah*. A similar scroll sits in front of each congregant. The *hazzan* begins the reading suddenly, chanting the text to a particular traditional melody. How artfully he interprets the most sublime passages of this curious, colorful story! How brilliantly he can convey every meaning, every nuance, like a first-rate actor using voice and body to bring out every line that the author wrote! When the *Megillah* describes Ahasuerus's banquet for all the nobles of his court, the sacred author says copious wine was served in opulent *"vessels of gold—the vessels being diverse one from the other.*" The *hazzan* chants these words in a sad, melancholy tone.

Were these not, after all, the same cups that the kings of Assyria pillaged long ago from the Temple in Jerusalem?

But his voice takes on such malice and comic verve when reading the famous scene of Haman's downfall, a scene that should serve as a lesson to any member of a royal court: For too long, the king had failed to reward the devotion of Mordecai the Jew, who had once saved him from a plot by two violent conspirators. Ahasuerus sent for Haman, his favorite and highest-ranking minister, to ask him what the king could do for a man worthy of the highest honors.

And Haman said in his heart, "Whom should the king desire to honor more than myself?" Haman therefore said to the king, "For the man whom the king desireth to honor, let him wear a royal apparel and ride a horse on which the king hath ridden, one with a royal crown upon its head, and let the grand marshal of the palace lead the horse through the streets of the city, and proclaim before him, 'Thus shall be done to the man whom the king desireth to honor.'" Then said the king to Haman, "Make haste, take the apparel and the horse, as thou hast spoken, and do thus to Mordecai the Jew, that sitteth at the king's gate: leave out nothing of all that thou hast spoken."

Caught in his own trap, Haman had to follow the order without complaining. And you should hear the *hazzan* when, in the amusingly ridiculous role of Haman, in front of this enraptured village congregation, he cries out the famous line, "Thus shall be done to the man whom the king desireth to honor!"

Later, after Esther denounces Haman to the king, Haman takes advantage of the king's brief absence from the banquet and begs for mercy at Esther's feet. The king returns suddenly and, seeing Haman reach towards the queen's couch, cries out, "Will he even do violence to the queen before me in the house?" The *hazzan* utters these words with a mix of contemptuous jealousy and husband-ly despotism, which makes the husbands in the congregation smile and the wives fume.

Is that all? Does the reading have no other notable features? It is our duty as a historian to mention one more. You have not forgotten our boys armed with wooden hammers, have you? There they wait, paying meticulous attention to the *hazzan*'s voice. Every time he utters the name of Haman, son of Hammedatha, you should see how, as one, they bend down and batter the synagogue floor with their hammers mercilessly for at least five minutes. These innumerable blows are understood to fall on Haman himself; the Jewish youth of our villages pay him this seasonal tribute every year in the same way. After more than 2,200 years of this punishment, if Ahasu-erus's former minister does not yet have a flattened back, we must agree it is not the fault of his young enemies and he must simply have strong shoulders.

After the *Megillah* reading, everyone goes home to break the fast. *Purim* has begun.

The next day at morning services, the *hazzan* reads the *Megillah* again with the same ceremony and same vocal inflections. And again at key moments, the tireless enemies of the Amalekite strike at Haman's imaginary back with all their might, and chant this verse from the book of Esther in chorus with the *hazzan*: "So they hanged Haman on the gallows which he had prepared for Mordecai."

Before leaving the synagogue, the crowd makes a point to walk past the Holy Ark, where the administrators have carefully placed two containers marked, respectively, *machtzei hashekel*[1] and *matnes Purim*.[2] In the first, the faithful deposit about 25 centimes apiece for the poor Jews of Palestine. In the other, they donate a sum proportional to their means or their goodwill, to benefit local needy brethren. Here again is the same spirit of charity we pointed out and admired elsewhere. On days of joy, they never forget their unfortunate fellow Jews!

Raucous, joyous *Purim* reigns everywhere now. Though Jewish law does not forbid work today, people set aside their business. As they await the evening's great Purim feast, which we shall describe soon, there are thousands of festive ways to spend the day. Delicious aromas from all kinds of pastry waft from every Jewish home, no matter how poor the inhabitants. The *Purim cakes* consist of babas, beignets and waffles, which everyone eats for breakfast. Then, if time permits, the older

[1] Translator's note: Or *machatzis hashekel* in Ashkenazic Hebrew, meaning "half a shekel."

[2] Translator's note: The original book says *mavet Purim*, which is surely an error. *Matnes Purim* is a stock phrase meaning "Purim donations."

boys leave the village to play a game of *bouchon* while the girls do some quick grooming and spend the morning chattering left and right.

The afternoon is spent making the rounds with *shlach moness*. What is *shlach moness*? You will see. The *Megillah* tells us that the Jews of Shushan, overjoyed at their miraculous deliverance, exchanged "portions" or gifts, and that Mordecai and Esther ordered all Jews to do the same thing down through the ages to commemorate *Purim*. Our villagers still follow this command to the letter. See the girls come and go in their holiday clothes, gracefully carrying green or brown faience plates covered with a white napkin. These are the daughters of well-off families, exchanging *shlach moness* with loved ones. All sorts of treats and candies make up these gifts, created in Colmar or Strasbourg (depending whether you live in Haut-Rhin or Bas-Rhin) and delivered fresh to the village that very morning. When choosing these presents, tradition leaves very little room for creativity. At least among the middle classes, the countless gifts given on this day are, if I may say so, endless variations on one theme. That theme is Savoy cakes of varying sizes in any of the following shapes: a melon with clearly defined slices, a dome, a star, a circle, a cone or a pyramid. At the same time, this custom offers a tactful way to give alms to the poor of a certain class without hurting their pride: Honoring the joyous *Purim* commandment, poor Jews begin making their own type of *shlach moness* the previous day to take to wealthy houses. When they return home, they always find a few silver coins under the napkin on their plate. The

Kugelhopf yeast cake, a *Purim* favorite in Alsace.

lady of the house had slipped them there after accepting the *shlach moness*, always with feigned admiration. The poor usually bring baked items shaped like people, or confections that look like glazed boots or shoes with red bows, or they give pralines, or the treats known as "shepherdesses" (*bergères*), or else candies wrapped in bits of paper with sayings on them. In exchange, the poor receive their "portion." That is, you will recall, what the book of Esther commanded.

Now daylight is gone. Night has taken the sky and in every well-to-do home, the *Purim* feast is being served and eaten. It consists of two distinct acts: In Act One, only the family appears, enjoying a comfortable dinner. Act Two is the party itself, because Mordecai and Esther ordered all Jews to make this "a day of entertainment and joy." The second round of food is not served until nine, once the usual guests have arrived: strangers, friends, neighbors, and in every wealthy home, a few dignitaries. This second seating features an indispensable dish called *Haman's plate* or simply the *Haman*: a thick chunk of very fatty smoked beef. All good believers are expected to have it served at their table, and all guests are expected to taste it. At one point, the *hazzan* and his apprentices arrive with the teacher and the *shammes*. They sit at the table, break bread, clink glasses, and get up again to do the same in many, many other homes. As public figures, they belong to no one in particular and are responsible to everybody. There is also a moment when the house, with its doors welcomingly open, is invaded by a surge of costumed youths. These fellows have come to sing a holiday song at poor Haman's expense. Then, with permission from the master of the house, some masqueraders step forward to give a dramatic performance. They take their places and the wandering troupe gives a fine rendering of the two usual plays, one of which is about *Purim* while the other tells a more generally Jewish story. The first is timely and well-suited to the holiday: the story of Esther and Mordecai's deliverance of the Jews, divided into several acts. The second play depicts the binding of Isaac as told in the Bible. The actors playing these historical figures show boundless energy and enthusiasm. Just picture Mordecai entering in royal attire, riding on the back of his friend who plays the horse. This beast of burden is led by another friend who, portraying the distraught Haman, chokes with shame and spite as he declaims in Hebrew, "Thus shall be done to the man whom the king desireth to honor!"

Also picture Abraham lifting a giant wooden knife to sacrifice his son, Isaac, who lies tied up across a chair. Imagine the actor playing the Angel of the Lord, running in not from the Heavens but from the end of the hallway where he has been hiding, racing in with paper wings sewn to his shoulders. Hear him proclaim (this time in *Yiddish*, in a tone meant to sound solemn), "Lay not thy hand upon thy son, and do him no harm, for now I know that thou fearest God, seeing that thou hast not withheld thy son, thine only one, from Him!"

Everyone applauds and the young troupe is given food and drink, including immense slices of *Haman* that they devour with sacred gluttony. Glasses are drained and promptly refilled and the mirth lasts long into the night, in keeping with the *Megillah*'s final recommendations:

> Mordecai ordered all the Jews to celebrate the fourteenth day of the month *Adar*, and the fifteenth day of the same in every year, like those days whereon the Jews had rest from their enemies, and the month which was changed unto them from sorrow to joy, and from mourning into a feast-day.

In each home, the feasts are so abundant that there is plenty left over the next day. Hence the Jewish country proverb, "Do you want to travel? Go the day after *Purim*." In other words, on that day among Jews everywhere, you will find good cheer and generosity.

CHAPTER TWO

Chanukah; its historical origin; a miracle. — Chanukah in Alsace; holiday lights in the synagogue and at home; various customs; the money known as Chanukah money; the Mo'oz Tsur. Chanukah evenings; visits; games; strange and profane coincidences: Saint Nicholas' Day and Christmas; refreshments. — Marriage interviews; delicate situations. — Fireside stories; Papa Roufenn. — An amazing tale.

WHO DOES NOT KNOW the story of the famous Maccabees, those heroes of Jewish independence in the days of the Second Temple, under the cruel domination of the Seleucid Empire? Who has not heard, especially, of the exploits of the bravest of the seven Hasmonean brothers: Judah, the rampart of Israel? For so many years, alas, Jerusalem, the holy city, was under the power of the Syrian kings, and the cult of pagan gods had replaced the worship of Jehovah in the Temple. But one day, the Maccabees rose up, inflamed with love for their God and country, frustrated at living under the yoke of their conquerors. They hoisted the banner of freedom and led a handful of equally determined men to defeat their more numerous enemies and free Jerusalem from the presence of the outsider.

Judah Maccabee destroyed the Gentiles' sacrificial altars, had the altar of the true God rebuilt, and replaced the sacred objects. He restored the sanctuary, purified the Temple and lit the lamps in its sacred front courtyards to the sound of the Levites' musical instruments and singing. This celebration—for it was a celebration—was called the *Festival of Dedication*, or in Hebrew, *Chanukah*. It lasted eight whole days and a great miracle happened: they had found just one single vial of holy oil but it lasted long enough to feed the golden lampstand for an entire week.

That is the historical and religious origin of the holiday of *Chanukah*, which is still observed faithfully in our market towns in the Haut-Rhin and Bas-Rhin regions. That famous rededication occurred on the 25th day of the month of *Kislev*, 164 years before the Common Era, at the same time of year when it is celebrated today. Now as then, it lasts eight days during which people can, in fact, work and go about their business.

The month of *Kislev* corresponds to December. Nature is again stripped of its finery and radiance. The wind blows and snow often falls. Tonight is the first night of *Chanukah*. The *Mincha* prayer is over. Holding a candle in his hand in front of the congregation, the *hazzan* (prayer leader) approaches a row of eight other candles with their wicks intact, and raises his voice.

"Blessed art Thou, O Lord our God," he says, "King of the Universe, who hath sanctified us with Thy commandments, and ordered us to light the lamps of *Chanukah*. Blessed art Thou, O Lord our God, King of the

Universe, who did miracles for our ancestors in times past at this season. Blessed art Thou, O Lord our God, King of the Universe, who in Thy mercy enabled us to reach this festival."

And he lights *one* of the candles in front of him. On the second evening he will light *two*, and so on until there are *eight*.

After synagogue, every family man will carry out the same ceremony at home, and any sons in the house will imitate their father. In every Jewish building this evening, a multitude of candles spreads brightness and joy everywhere. This is in memory of the lights the Maccabees lit after restoring the Temple. Those who can afford it use a special silver candelabrum shaped to look as much as possible like the seven-branched lampstand. These are used only one week a year, but rich families consider them an indispensable household item, handed down as a sacred heirloom from generation to generation.

Children jump and dance in the splendidly lit rooms. Moments later they approach their parents, holding out one hand. The parents understand and drop some coins into the open palm, proportional to the supplicants' age and merit. People give *Chanukah money* because for the next eight days, everyone must have fun—old and young, men and women—and especially everyone must play games. Among our country Jews, gambling is an essential pastime on this holiday, as we shall see.

First, everyone in every home enjoys a succulent meal in which smoked meat is the traditional main course.

A father chants the *Chanukah* prayers
and his little son repeats them.

Then everybody leaves the table. In the parlor, everything is tidy and pretty, almost as it would be on a Sabbath Eve.

Friends and neighbors will arrive in a few seconds, visiting one home after another to play games, chat or find other diversions.

But listen! Someone is knocking at the door. The dog barks and the door opens. A man in a hat and cloak enters carrying a lantern, stations himself near the stove, and in a fairly pleasing voice, sings a song in Hebrew. He is usually some retired *hazzan* or some poor rabbi, regaling his audience with the *Mo'oz Tzur*.

This is the name of an old poem that lists the ills that befell our ancestors, from the Exodus to the persecutions by Antiochus, and all the miracles that God unceasingly worked to free us from tyrants.

He reels off this song to a specific bright, lively tune, well known throughout Jewish Alsace.

The deed done, the singer relights his lantern (which he had extinguished on arrival) and makes sure to walk past the master of the house, who pays him for his trouble. Our man then continues his tour of the village.

Bursts of fresh, gleeful laughter announce the imminent arrival of male and female neighbors, men, young women and girls, coming to celebrate *Chanukah*. They are dressed for a secondary holiday: men in a frock coat or velvet jacket and a cap, women in a merino wool dress with a black taffeta apron. Married women wear their usual velvet "wrap" that stands in for their hair, and on top of this sits a tulle bonnet laden with bright ribbons. A watch-guard chain hangs around their neck. Young girls' hair is exposed, and in place of neckerchiefs they wear thin scarves with large floral patterns.

In a corner of the room, groups of children play *trenderl*.[1] The grown-ups are no less busy: here, they play a game of *bête*; over there, a game of *rams*; further down, *valet* and *as*; and still further along, around the big freshly waxed walnut table in the center of the room, with its huge brass candlesticks and snuffers, they play a raucous game of *reschoussé*. This is like a village version of the card game *lansquenet*, and is, by the way, highly popular and respected, but only among rural Jews.

After a quarter of an hour, the excitement is at its peak. The laughter and the cries of triumph or misfortune are deafening.

Every so often, though, the tumult stops suddenly for a few minutes. This happens when a sound comes from the street: sometimes the clank of chains and little bells mixed with confused shouting, sometimes the bellowing of heifers and milk cows, or the neighing of horses preceded by or followed by the crack of whips. — What is it? Well, because *Chanukah* falls in December, it often coincides either with St. Nicholas' Day or with Christmas Eve. Among our Christian neighbors in the village, St. Nicholas (patron saint of little boys) can take horrifying forms. He arrives not as a saint but as a devil: eyes ablaze, black beard, a pitchfork in his hand, hurtling into the street

---

[1] *Trenderls* are like dice that spin on a point for a long time, decorated with Hebrew letters indicating whether the player won or lost. [Translator's note: I.e., *dreidels*.]

through a terrified crowd, banging the pavement with pieces of iron and beating out a rhythm on the broken remains of bells to inspire healthy fear among disobedient little brats. — Christmas Eve is a different matter. At midnight precisely, herders and plowboys take all the residents of the stables and cowsheds to the village's big watering trough. Atop this watering place is a statue of the holy Virgin. On that night, through pipes that feed the vast stone basin, the Virgin is kind enough to send not water, if you please, but streams of an admittedly invisible excellent red wine meant for the local four-legged creatures alone, which is sure to give them strength and health. — But we have wandered far afield from our Jewish *Chanukah*. Let us hurry back.

At midnight, the games stop and refreshments arrive: The lady of the house herself brings in baskets of apples, pears, nuts and grapes. A big loaf of brown bread is placed in the middle of the table, and white wine of the latest vintage is poured from elegant terra-cotta pitchers.

Some nights during this eight-day holiday are filled not with games but with conversation. This is especially true in homes with a marriageable young daughter, who—given the leisures of *Chanukah*, a sort of winter *Chol Hamoed*—expects a visit from her suitor that very evening. They will have what is known as a *frayeray*: a marriage interview. The family is ready for battle. The suitor, who has been staying with a friend in the village for the past twenty-four hours, presents himself at the agreed time accompanied by the *shadshen* (matchmaker). Supposedly, it is just a social call to pay his respects to the family. That poor suitor. They are polite to him, it is true, but how they look him up and down! How they question him! How endlessly they scrutinize him! It is his job to please not only the young woman but also her father, mother, grandparents, aunt and cousins. Anyone lacking self-confidence might be petrified! This ordeal has been known to bewilder some boys so thoroughly that, after standing twenty minutes in front of a red-hot stove or opposite a wooden bench, the shy lad can think of nothing to say but "This fire is hot" or "That bench is hard." The assemblage has no choice but to look at each other, the *shadshen* no choice but to leave without a word, and the young man no choice but to hastily try to discover the young beauty's intentions.

Other times it is the girl who is at a loss, especially if her education was lacking or if nature did not endow her with great intelligence, or if, as is common among our people, she is not fluent in the national language and must talk with a French-speaking suitor.

If both parties agree, then on that same *Chanukah* night, the young man's parents come to join them, the scribe is sent for to draw up the *tenoim* (contract), and they *break the cup* to consummate the betrothal. A great meal follows, the hamlet rejoices, and the locals have a topic of conversation for at least eight days.

As we mentioned, the entertainment in Jewish homes varies on different days of *Chanukah*. Some nights there is neither gambling nor idle chatter. What do people do? They amuse themselves in a different way. And what does this new pleasure consist of? Simply this: You gather a large

Matchmaking.

group at someone's home to hear an Alsatian storyteller
such as Samuel spin tales as only these past masters of
such yarns can do, with peerless eloquence and appeal.
Of course these stories will deal exclusively with Jewish
subjects, usually drawn from medieval annals, and will
often emphasize the supernatural. We are in the parlor.
Chanukah lights shine all around and the stove murmurs
as the north wind shakes the shutters outside. From time
to time, we hear the tinkle of bells outdoors followed by a
shrill sound: a sleigh riding over hardened snow on the
main street. Everyone huddles with increasing pleasure
around the storyteller, whom the master of the house has
hired as the evening's recreation. His repertoire is limit-
less! He especially loves to evoke memories of certain
glorious German *kehillahs* in the olden days, transporting
his listeners to Frankfurt, to Worms or to Prague. Frankfurt! Worms! Prague! These cities always had sizable
Jewish populations, including famous Kabbalistic rabbis
who had witnessed many bizarre occurrences. Sometimes
these rabbis took part in mysterious events themselves,
but more often they exorcised them: newborns torn from
mothers by midwife-witches disguised as evil animals;
Asmodeus stirring up mischief in a pious household that
forgot to place protective *mezuzahs* in the necessary spot;
rabbis' daughters abducted by *sheydim* (demons) and
transported to marvelous palaces at the bottom of the
River Rhine, or the River Moldau, or the Main, and res-
cued miraculously! Stories of automatons brought to life
through Kabbalistic formulas placed under their tongue
by sage rabbis, to be the rabbis' docile slaves; epidemics

sent by an angry Heaven "to punish the crimes of the Earth," dispelled at last through the wisdom or courage of this or that religious leader of the community. Such are the thousands of subjects that inspire our storytellers. I mentioned epidemics a moment ago, which reminds me of a childhood memory I would like to share with you.

We were in my father's house one *Chanukah* evening, gathered around a familiar guest in our home: old Roufenn. He had been the teacher of our friend Samuel and was a fellow storyteller. Like Samuel, he excelled at recounting fantastical, wonderful tales. The setting was long ago in Prague and the hero was Rabbi Loew—the *Great Rabbi Loew*, as people still call him. He was a contemporary and friend of King Rudolph II of Bohemia and of the famous astronomer Tycho Brahe. If only I could let you hear Roufenn speak in the frank, expressive Alsatian *Yiddish* that rang in our ears that night, which I can still hear today! You would enjoy it all the more, but alas, on the one hand, most people cannot understand this Jewish patois, and on the other, it is sadly untranslatable. So I shall merely reconstruct and report—as best I can, and in pale language—Roufenn's vivid, colorful, imaginative story. And with your kind permission, we shall leave you with the impression of this one last memory of the nights of an Alsatian *Chanukah*.

"It was during the reign of Rudolph II. A horrible epidemic suddenly struck the Jews of Prague. That scourge —this is true—spared the men, women and youths, but punished the children mercilessly. Thousands of these poor little creatures, innocent of all sin and misdeed, fell daily to the cruel treacheries of Death. In the streets, you saw nothing but funeral processions going to the *beys-hayim* (cemetery) of the Jewish community. Sometimes, countless little corpses piled up for days until they could be buried, for there were not enough arms to dig graves for so many victims, all taken tragically at a tender age. These piles of bodies gave off miasmas that made the plague still worse. Everywhere in the city, you heard only wailing and lamentation and saw parents with their clothing torn as a sign of mourning, crying out in despair as they followed the coffins of their dear little ones. Flocks of grieving siblings roamed the ghetto, weeping for their young brothers and sisters whom death kept stealing one after the other. Strangely, the ravages of this plague affected only the Jewish quarter! There alone did people die; none died elsewhere. The wrath of Heaven, it seemed, was aimed solely at the children of Israel! Clearly, in their midst, some great sin was being committed or had been committed, and until there was atonement, the whole community would pay with what they held dearest: their children, joy of the present and hope of the future. At this distressing juncture, on orders from the head of the *kehillah*, the Jews gathered in their synagogues and prayed for God to lift the plague from His people, and they fasted and did penance. In vain! The demand for gravediggers increased daily. Then all of Prague's rabbis and *Talmudists* (Talmud scholars) met to deliberate. How could they exorcise this evil and end the torment? How could they restrain the tireless arm of Death from striking blow after blow without end?

They pondered at length, wondering what failure, what sin, what crime had caused Heaven to punish the Jews. But the rabbis and sages of Prague tortured their minds for nothing, for they could not learn the cause of this evil.

"That night, they went their separate ways. Their learned group included a man universally celebrated for his deep, vast knowledge. This man, whom people praised to the skies, was the Rabbi of Prague himself, the illustrious Rabbi Loew. Back home, he tossed and turned in bed, overwhelmed by sadness and insomnia. Whenever he thought of all the parents who at that moment were surely sitting on the edge of their dear child's deathbed, the *Rav* (Rabbi) sighed a long sigh from the depths of his heart and wept bitterly. Then all at once he raised up his soul to the God of Israel and asked Him, for the hundredth time, to shine a ray of grace on His servant and show him the cause of this misery looming over the *kehillah*. Soon the rabbi fell asleep and had a dream. He dreamed it was midnight and he thought he saw the prophet Elijah approaching to lead him to the cemetery, where they both watched ghostly children emerge from their graves. Just then the rabbi awoke and thought about that strange dream for a long time...

"Who knows? Maybe God in His mercy sent him that dream to point him to the knowledge he needed: the cause of this public calamity. And the pious rabbi thanked Heaven effusively for the favor it had just shown him. He soon made use of it. He sent urgently for one of his *bochrim* (disciples), the one he considered bravest and strongest of character. The *bocher* (disciple) appeared promptly.

"'Listen,' the rabbi said, 'God is punishing us cruelly because we have sinned. Now we must find out what our crime is. So summon all your courage, and tonight as midnight approaches, go to the cemetery. Soon you will see the recently dead children come out of their graves clad in their *tachrichim* (shrouds). Try to snatch the *tachrichim* from one of them and bring it to me at once.'

"The *bocher* obeyed the rabbi's orders. Towards midnight he went to the graveyard, nervously awaiting the predicted apparition. The night was beautiful: millions of stars shone in the firmament and the cemetery was deathly silent. Only occasionally, he heard the heavy wings of a bat or the sound of wind whistling through the leaves of the trees planted on the graves. About half an hour later, the clock on the Jewish community hall struck twelve. The twelfth stroke had scarcely faded when everything began to move under the grave markers. Small children began to appear, wrapped in white linin. They glided over the graves for a few moments and then started ed dancing a most unusual dance! The dance of the dead. At this sight, the *bocher* shuddered. Sweat beaded on his brow and all his limbs shook. But didn't his entire community's happiness and peace depend now on his courage alone? That thought brought him back to his senses. In one leap, he bounded into that line of little phantoms, grabbed the *tachrichim* from a child and ran back to the rabbi with it. Rabbi Loew sat by his window, awaiting his disciple. The student, still out of breath, told him what had happened and handed him the *tachrichim* he had stripped from the child. Seconds later, the rabbi saw the stark-naked ghost of a little boy rush through the streets, quick as an arrow. This made sense. The spirits had kept dancing until the clock struck one, and then returned to their graves. Only then did the boy realize he no longer had his shroud, and without his shroud he could not return to his coffin. He therefore flew swiftly to the rabbi's house. Under the window, he held out his little hands pleadingly towards the rabbi and shed bitter tears.

"'Rabbi,' he sobbed, 'give me back my *tachrichim*.'

"'I'll give back your *tachrichim* but only if you do as I say. Tell me, then, the cause of this epidemic that God has set loose on us. What crime does He seek to punish?'

"The child kept silent. He would not explain but again started to request, beg, implore the rabbi's pity. Alas, the hour had passed. All his little companions were at rest again and only he, deprived of his shroud, could not return to the grave. But his pleading and supplications were useless.

"'Once again, tell me,' the rabbi replied. 'Why is God punishing us so harshly and what crime have we committed to warrant such a penalty? Tell me and I will return your *tachrichim*.'

"The child resisted for a long time. Finally, seeing that the rabbi would not yield, the boy told him the secret cause of the epidemic ravaging the ghetto: On a street very near the rabbi's home, two married couples lived under one roof and had the most immoral relations with each other. It was a disgrace for the Jewish people, a scandal for the religion. Therefore the epidemic would continue to rage and take innocent victims until the culprits were duly punished.

"'And now that I have done as you said,' the child added, 'give me back my *tachrichim*.'

"'How do I know this revelation is true,' the rabbi asked, 'and not a trick to get back your *tachrichim*? I'll go see for myself whether you've told the truth, and if so, I'll return your shroud.'

"The rabbi got up and, accompanied by the boy, went to the house in question. He quickly saw that the child was not wrong and returned his garment. The boy, very pleased to have his shroud, hastened back to the cemetery to lie again in his grave and sleep his eternal rest. The rabbi ordered due punishment of the two couples who had brought such a calamity down on the *kehillah*. How many families had paid with bereavement and how many poor little tots had paid with their lives for the misdeeds of the guilty! And at that moment, the epidemic ceased its ravages."

Dear reader, I am sure you do not doubt the truth of this tale that I heard years ago from Papa Rouffenn. If you do have qualms, you can settle them easily: just go to Prague, find the community's *shammes* (beadle) and ask him to take you to a certain street in the ghetto: *Bel-El Street*. That is what people called the street where the two guilty couples once lived, since one woman punished by Rabbi Loew was called *Beyla* and the other *Ella*, which are still extremely common names for women among

Jewish families in Germany and Alsace. However, out of respect for Alsatian mores, and to paraphrase two famous pieces of verse, I hurry to add that in our communities:

> The names are common
> But the things named are rare.

THE END

Bibliography

Timeline of these stories

1849–53: "Lettres sur les mœurs alsaciennes" (Letters on Alsatian customs). Serialized in *Archives Israélites*, 10 (1849): 643–56; 11 (1850): 72–87, 246–51, 425–32, 465–69; 12 (1851): 65–71, 95–99, 204–09, 461–68; 13 (1852): 627–36, 689–96; 14 (1853): 374–83.

An early, significantly different version of the first half of the book, aimed specifically at a Jewish readership. The present English translation relied on these stories only for the Yiddishisms and other Jewish terms that Widal later deleted when revising them for a mainstream audience.

1857–59: "Scènes de la vie juive en Alsace" (Scenes of Jewish life in Alsace). In *Revue des Deux Mondes*, 10 (1857): 345–376; 24 (1859): 124–152.

Revisions of the *Archives Israélites* stories plus new tales about the spring and autumn Jewish holidays. Besides strengthening the structure of the stories, Widal strove to make them more understandable to Gentile readers. This was the first version to appear under the pseudonym Daniel Stauben.

1860:   *Scènes de la vie juive en Alsace* (Scenes of Jewish life in Alsace). Paris: Michel Lévy Frères, 1860.

This book was the final and longest version, including several new stories. Published under the pseudonym Daniel Stauben, it was the main French source for the present English translation.

Other Sources

Cahun, Léon. *La vie juive*. Paris: Ed. Monnier, De Brunhoff et Cie., 1886. A similar collection of stories about Jewish life in nineteenth-century Alsace. Besides its charm as a work of fiction, it is of interest for its occasional phonetic renderings of Alsatian Yiddish and Hebrew. It was the source for many of the Lévy illustrations used in the present volume.

De Sola, Abraham, D. A. De Sola, Isaac Leeser and Benjamin Artom, eds. *Day of Atonement Service*, vol. 3 of *The Form of Prayers According to the Custom of the Spanish and Portuguese Jews*. Philadelphia: Sherman & Co., 5638 [1877–78].

Leeser, Isaac, trans. *The Twenty-Four Books of the Holy Scriptures*. Philadelphia: Leeser, 1853.

Lévy, Alphonse. *Scènes familiales juives*. Paris: Felix Juven, [1902]. Picture plates of more than twenty Lévy illustrations of Jewish life in Alsace.

Mendes, A. P. *Service for the First Nights of Passover According to the Custom of the German and Polish Jews*. London: P. Vallentine, 1862.

Polano, H., trans. and ed. *The Talmud: Selections from the Contents of That Ancient Book, Its Commentaries, Teachings, Poetry and Legends*. London: Federick Warne and Co., 1876.

Samuels, Maurice. *Inventing the Israelite: Jewish Fiction in Nineteenth-Century France*. Stanford, CA: Stanford University Press, 2010. Includes background on Widal and his place in nineteenth-century French Jewish literature.

"Yédisch-Daïtsch: Le dialecte judéo-alsacien," Site du Judaïsme d'Alsace et de Lorraine, accessed May 19, 2018. http://judaisme.sdv.fr/dialecte/. This is the language section of a website about Judaism in Alsace and Lorraine. It includes glossaries, phonetic renderings and descriptive material about Alsatian Yiddish, much of it compiled by local rabbis from the 1840s to 2010s.

Zuckerman, Richard. "Alsace: An Outpost of Western Yiddish." In *The Field of Yiddish: Studies in Language, Folklore, and Literature, Third Collection*, edited by Marvin I. Herzog, Wita Ravid and Uriel Weinreich, 36–57. London: Mouton & Co., 1969. A phonological analysis of Alsatian Yiddish, based on Zuckerman's fieldwork in Alsace in 1963 and 1964.

Translator's Acknowledgments

SOME VERY KIND PEOPLE made this a much better book. Mitchell Bloom's eye for good writing helped to clarify the wording, eliminate inconsistencies and delete surplus punctuation. In addition, his professional expertise in historical clothing kept the descriptions of period fabrics and clothes accurate and clear. Amanda Miryem-Khaye Seigel, that wonderful Yiddishist–librarian–singer, gave cheerful encouragement and invaluable information about Yiddish, and pointed out when my transliterations varied from chapter to chapter. Allan Altman's knowledge of orthodox Jewish practice and liturgy proved a great asset during revisions. His questions helped tighten the text and his feedback led to several footnotes. J. R. Wilheim gave solid feedback on the preface. The Yiddish scholar Alec Leyzer Burko, who I happened to sit next to at a cultural Seder, graciously emailed me the next day about resources on Yiddish dialectology and Alsatian Yiddish.

Some passages in this translation are the work of eloquent translators from the past. Whenever the author quoted French editions of the Bible, Talmud or prayers, I quoted or adapted text from nineteenth-century English editions: Isaac Leeser's *The Twenty-Four Books of the Holy Scriptures* (1853); H. Polano's *The Talmud: Selections from the Contents of That Ancient Book* (1876); A. P.

Mendes' *Service for the First Nights of Passover According to the Custom of the German and Polish Jews* (1862); and, when Widal quoted a French Sephardic Machzor, I turned to the 1870s revised edition of *Form of Prayers According to the Custom of the Spanish and Portuguese Jews: Day of Atonement Service*, translated by Isaac Leeson, D. A. de Sola and others.

The main sources for the Alphonse Lévy illustrations were Léon Cahun's 1886 book *La vie juive*, Lévy's 1902 art book *Scènes familiales juives*, and a series of Lévy postcards published around 1900. The lithograph in the final chapter, *Shiddukh (The Engagement)*, is held by the University of Chicago Library. The one non-Lévy illustration, the portrait of Rabbi Hirsch, comes from an anonymous nineteenth-century print held by the Bibliothèque Nationale et Universitaire de Strasbourg. As for the front cover design (also derived from a Lévy illustration), it was something of a team effort: I came up with a rough concept, James Rollins Designs patiently and creatively turned it into something infinitely better, and many of my friends and relatives, including my parents and brother, looked at the options James sent and made suggestions and recommendations.

Lastly, a big thank you to everyone who bought the previous books in the Between Wanderings collection: *Sephardic Jews and the Spanish Language* by Ángel Pulido, and the photo booklet *Jewish Immigrants in Early 1900s America* with text by Anatole Leroy-Beaulieu. Thanks to your support, the next two volumes are already in progress.

ABOUT THE AUTHOR

C. AUGUSTE WIDAL (1822–1875, a.k.a. "Daniel Stauben") was born in Wintzenheim in the Alsace region of eastern France. He studied in Colmar and Paris and spent his professional life as a professor of classics and modern languages at various French universities. His scholarly writings include books about Juvenal, Seneca and Homer, and about the figure of the misanthrope in ancient and modern literature.

Widal's "Letters on Alsatian Customs" began appearing in the Jewish magazine *Archives Israélites* in 1849. He later revised them and added new stories to the series for the literary and cultural magazine *Revue des Deux Mondes* under the title "Scenes of Jewish Life in Alsace." His 1860 book of the same title expanded the existing tales and added new ones. He used the pen name Daniel Stauben for the *Revue* stories and the book, and for his French translations of Leopold Kompert's Jewish story collections *Aus dem Ghetto* (In the ghetto) and *Böhmische Juden* (Jews of Bohemia). Widal died in Paris at the age of fifty-three.

ABOUT THE TRANSLATOR

STEVEN CAPSUTO (b. 1964) translates the Between Wanderings book series and edits the Between Wanderings blog, which focus on Jewish social history and culture from the 1850s to 1920s. He grew up in the Philadelphia area in a part-Sephardic, part-Ashkenazic family and now lives in New York City.

Steven studied translation at Rutgers University and has been a full-time translator since 2003, working from Spanish, French, Catalan, Portuguese and Ladino into English. Professionally, he has translated stage plays, economic forecasts, biomedical texts, family records, websites, corporate newsletters, technical manuals and many other types of documents. He holds certifications in three language pairs from the American Translators Association.

He is also a nonfiction author: Steven's media-history book *Alternate Channels* was a semifinalist for an American Library Association book award in 2001.

For more information about these books and about Jewish culture and history, visit the

Between Wanderings blog:
betweenwanderings.com

Twitter: @BWJewishHistory

CPSIA information can be obtained
at www.ICGtesting.com
Printed in the USA
FSHW021257200720
72308FS